Shadow on the Sea

S.J. GARRETT

For all those who believe that love is the greatest gift of all, this is for you.

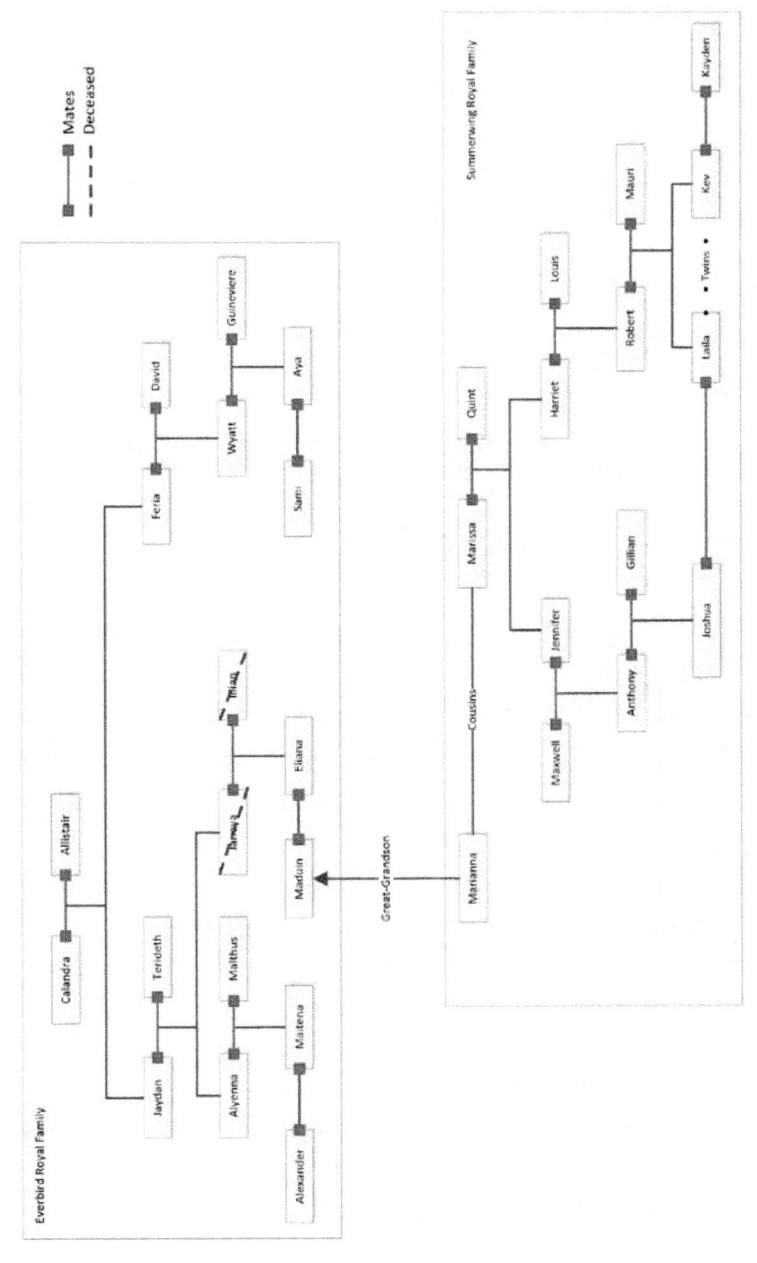

1
Shadow on the Rise

The world of Ceres ran parallel to Earth in what could be considered another dimension and yet was not truly so. Earth did not really know of its existence at all. It had been born when the powers of Light and Dark crossed and brought life where there had been none before. Across the surface of Ceres lived many humans, and a powerful race known simply as Lightlings.

Lightlings had once been humans. Some children had been born with souls so light, so beautiful, that they grew shimmering wings. The beauty radiated out of their very souls with a force that transcended gender so that all who viewed them were left breathless. Some Lightlings had gone to Earth over the centuries, and they had sparked the legend of angels. In humor and appreciation for such a thing, the race had officially adopted the nickname.

Yet, Lightlings were not the only winged race of Ceres. They had a dark cousin known, appropriately, as Darklings. The Darklings had appeared as a genetic mutation in pureblooded families some few hundred years before. Both halves of the angelic race were nearly identical in all ways; they differed only in the element of their birth, the color of their wings, and the natural gift of those with wings. An angel who was Light, white, and had lightning was a Lightling. An angel who was Dark, black, and had fire was a Darkling.

Darklings were not as populous as their cousins, though they were common enough. The Darkling gene was recessive and always overridden by Lightling genes if the two were paired together. It was a situation not aided by both sides of the angelic genus being less fertile than most other mammalian species. Angels were born with only one soul mate—a destined mate—and they were only capable of producing children with that mate. Their wings, that thing that made them beautiful and powerful, was also their weakness. Making love with wings exposed could dramatically increase an angel's fertility, but an angel only ever gave their wings to their mate.

Still, as the dawning of a new century began, both species were safely populous enough to not quite be endangered. Nature and Destiny both loved angels, and Ceres would always find a way to keep the two species alive. It was a situation aided by the royal families who were known for often managing more than one child per generation. There were two kingdoms on Ceres, those of Chalice and Crystal, and theirs were the oldest and most powerful of all angelic bloodlines.

Queen Alyenna Everbird ruled over Chalice with her husband, Malthus. The dawning of the new century was bringing an increase to their family as well, for Alyenna was heavily pregnant with a daughter. She kept her ears open for every bit of legend and story she could since her child would be born into a changing era. Rumor had begun to speculate about a coming prophecy: the return of the legendary Elemines.

Ceres, so blessed with magic, was protected by the six elemental beings known as Elemines. Their temple could be seen on the landscape though no mortals had been able to get close. Yet, there was a rumor, a prophecy that said there were two final Elemines known as Infinity and Shadow. What might be crumbled ruins of ancient temples implied it could be more than rumor, but there was no knowing how things would play out. Only if a child were ever born with Shadow or Infinity as their element would understanding begin to arrive.

When Alyenna was barely weeks away from delivery, the rumors picked up in force. Elemental power had been moving under the surface of the land. People whispered that the Shadow Elemine was to be reborn soon. Just twelve years before, Infinity elemental power had moved under the land as well, sparking thought that the Infinity Elemine would be reborn. No child had come forward as an Infinity element, yet people still wondered.

Really, Alyenna did not have much time left to wonder about anything except her family. She had a daughter coming soon, and she was also raising her young niece. The little Darkling had lost her parents to a quake, and Alyenna and Malthus had adamantly refused to let anyone else take in the baby angel. She was barely a few months old; she needed her real family.

Luckier still for the royal couple, they had lucked out in already finding her a guardian. Guardians were men and women, normally humans, who were blessed from birth with special gifts and skills that allowed them to protect and care for angels whose many powers and gifts could make them just as fragile. Alyenna and Malthus shared a guardian, a woman named

Talia who had already decreed she would not guard their daughter. She refused to get more gray hair than Alyenna had already given her.

Alyenna took the teasing in stride. She loved her guardian a great deal. At nineteen, she had been with her guardian since she was five and her guardian was sixteen. She truly, deeply, wished to give her daughter and niece the gift of having a guardian from birth. There was nothing like a guardian's unconditional love.

Eliana, her niece, had a guardian who was also a Darkling. It happened rarely, but did happen, that an angel of either color would become a guardian themselves. In fact, there was often only one condition that sparked it, but that was for Eliana to discover as she grew up. Maduin Grimoire, though just seven, was already partway through his needed training and was very protective and possessive of his little princess.

Alyenna had her eye on someone else entirely for her daughter. She had been eyeing the boy since she had discovered she was pregnant. He was just now twelve, and his father was an ambassador between the kingdoms. His young age in no way stopped him from being alarmingly skilled in multiple forms of combat; a true necessity in a world whose magic had creature all manner of feral beasts that most Earthlings would call monsters, but Cerelians just called annoying.

When it was truly only a matter of days, Alyenna finally sent a message to the boy's father to request the young guardian's presence. Her first clue that he would, indeed, be perfect was that she did not even hear his approach in the garden until he cleared his throat. She immediately looked over her shoulder and smiled. "Hello, Alexander. Come sit with me."

Alexander Solomon had grown up in the courts. He was already trained in the etiquette and manners suiting a courtier. He bowed gracefully and then walked over to sit beside the queen on the bench. He eyed her very pregnant belly intently and then told her, "She is restless."

"Ah, you have magic as well." Only magic would have sensed the agitation of her unborn child who was, indeed, restless and cranky. The moment an angel was conceived, it had a mind and soul. Alyenna had been communicating with her daughter for all of her pregnancy, and even Malthus had spoken with her. Fathers of angels could reach their children, too. "What is your element, Alexander?"

He hesitated. "We call it the Moon."

She arched a royal brow. "But it is not *actually* the Moon element?"

"No, Majesty. We don't truly know what it is, but I am capable of using spells of all elements. Sand, Air, Fire, Water, Sun, and Moon. I can access them all, but, my preference is for Moon."

She studied his violet eyes, and the way they shifted color with his mood, and just smiled to herself. The color of the Moon element was purple. "Ah, well, perhaps someday we will know more. The magic on Ceres is a curious thing. Not everyone has it though everyone still has an elemental power." She tilted her head. "What do you know of angels?"

"A bit," he admitted readily. "I have been studying them since I was old enough to read. Father always told me I had guardian gifts, and I want to use them. I wish to be a guardian someday, though I admit I'm not entirely sure what it means to be one."

"Allow me to help," she offered on a smile. "Angels are separated into three classes from birth. The two most common are Wizard and Warrior. Warriors are of exceptional strength, and they cannot use magic. On the other hand, Wizards possess exceptional magic and their strength lacks. I am a Wizard. My husband is a Warrior. Little Eliana is a Wizard. Joshua, the heir of the Crystal Kingdom, is a Warrior."

"And what will our princess be?"

"Special." She rested a hand on her belly. "One in a thousand, you will find a Shaman.

They are both Warrior and Wizard; they have the strength and magic both. Their powers harmonize with life itself and give them a beautiful music inside their hearts. It is through this music that they fully utilize their magic, and many other gifts even other Wizards cannot use."

"I see," he said slowly. "She will need a guardian who can use magic." Not all guardians had magic. Not all needed it.

"She will need a guardian who can use magic and who is quite strong within his or her own right." She sighed. "She will need a guardian who is also stubborn, strong willed, and perhaps a bit devilish as well. She is going to be a terror, Alexander, in the best of ways. I'm afraid she is much like her mother: she will want to always have her way. She will be perhaps a bit of a smartass, and she will love unconditionally in a way that will bruise her heart easily. Her magic feels as if it should rightfully belong to a healer, and they are unfailingly gentle."

"You have picked me." It wasn't a question because he knew well he wouldn't be there otherwise.

"I have." She put a hand on his shoulder. "But that is merely because I think you are perfect. Sitting here with you, I am more certain. Your presence has calmed her. But I cannot merely ask you to just blithely agree. What binds a guardian and an angel is a beautiful, profound thing. It is a great deal of love." She took a very long breath. "And it may result in the guardian doing something that will be the hardest thing in their life."

He looked up quickly. "What?"

She curled her hands together. "Alexander, you know that angels only have one destined mate." He nodded, and she closed her eyes. "Destined mates cannot be apart against their will. Even voluntarily can be excruciating. We enter into what is known as Angelic Separation. I could call it depression, but it would not encompass the agony we endure every second. It is the double-edged sword of the glory we feel when we are with our mate." Tears glimmered across her eyes. "Alexander . . . if one half of a mated pair dies, the other will enter into Separation and never emerge. They will stop eating. Sleeping. They will not smile or laugh. They will barely breathe. Their souls will slowly corrode and dissolve until the feathers fall from their wings and the wings break off entirely."

His stomach churned. "They'll die."

"If they are lucky. Otherwise it is nothing but an endless sea of suffering. A guardian . . ." She took a deep breath. "A guardian's ultimate duty is to—to kill their angel if the angel's mate dies. To end their suffering before it is too late and their halo breaks." A tear slid slowly down her cheek. "I saw it. Talia . . . Talia had to end my sister's Separation when her mate was killed in that quake. And when I saw how pitifully grateful Janeya was to reach her end, I finally understood how Talia could bear it."

"That is why we must love our angel," he realized very softly. "We must love them enough to kill them if needed." He drew a long breath. It was a daunting realization, but it seemed to explain why such powerful beings needed guardians at all. "What of angels who are mated to humans? Do humans suffer Separation?"

"They do, unfortunately. A human who is the destined mate of an angel has a soul not much less in beauty than their mate. To suddenly lose their angel would devastate them no less. They might be able to hang on during Separation a little longer, but they, too, would waste away. The angel's guardian would mercifully save them as needed. That is why a guardian is often shared between two angels, or an angel and their mate."

"And if a guardian *is* the mate of their angel? It happens, right?"

"It does, and actually more often than most realize. It is one of the reasons why some guardians find themselves with more than one angel they can love. Eliana and Maduin will be that way." She said it confidently. "Angelic bonds can form even as children and will grow until the angel reaches final maturity at eighteen and their soul fully develops to entirely support the force and fury of their emotions. Already I can see the bond forming between Eliana and her dark guardian. Should the unbearable happen and Eliana lost, Maduin would need to turn to a fellow guardian to save him."

He said slowly, "So if I was to be your daughter's guardian, I would someday need to guard whomever her mate turned out to be. What if her mate has a guardian? She is to be betrothed to Joshua, isn't she?"

"Anthony and I hope so anyway. Until he met Gillian, he and I were betrothed ourselves. We have discussed giving up if this generation does not work as well. There are other ways to cement our alliance through blood. Perhaps it will fall to Eliana and Maduin to be the tie; Maduin is of Summerwing blood as well, though a generation or two removed." She shook it off. "As for Josh, as of this moment, he does not have a guardian himself. His parents are looking, but, well, as I said. You can't pick just anyone. Should one be found for him, and he were to be my daughter's mate, you would share duties with his guardian."

It was a lot to think about. He had always loved angels of both colors, and he had been glad to have guardian gifts. He still felt that way. Perhaps a bit more honored, in fact, that he would be born capable of protecting such fascinating creatures. "I will accept the task of being your daughter's guardian *if* I love her the way I should when I meet her."

Her smile looked almost secretive. "I cannot ask for more, Alexander. She is to be born within a week, at most. I would ask that you take up residence within the palace and turn yourself over to Talia for training." She grinned briefly. "She knows me so well, she will be able to prepare you for my child." She laughed. "Everyone is so worried about my personality that they just don't realize Malthus' sheer tenacity and tendency to speak his mind is what they *really* should watch for!"

Alexander took up immediate residence in the palace, and Talia was more than glad to start training him. She was more bemused than vexed when he promptly proved to already be on her level. Her seventeen extra years in no way gave her an advantage. She took it for a sign that the princess would be vastly more troublesome than her mother. She also did not doubt that Alexander would be the princess' guardian. Alyenna wouldn't make that mistake.

One week later, while the rest of Ceres watched a rare but fascinating eclipse where the

Earth blocked the sun, the high princess and heir to the throne of the Chalice Kingdom was born kicking, screaming, and generally unhappy with the entire birth process. Her Shaman power was clear from the get-go for anyone who heard her unhappy cries felt utterly miserable as well. Neither her temperamental personality nor her Shaman voice were at all a surprise.

What *was* a surprise was that she did not resonate with the normal Light power she should have gotten from her parents. She also did not seem to resonate a Dark power that might have implied an unexpected, yet relatively natural, inheritance of the recessive Darkling genes that had made Alyenna's sister a Darkling as well. Nearly all Lightlings by that date had a recessive Dark gene *somewhere*.

Instead, the newborn angel seemed to be resonating *both*. There would be no way of knowing just what it all meant until her wings finally broke in at or around the age of two years. It did not really matter what power blessed her for she was still, clearly, an angel. The sunlight that poured in the window illuminated a fierce and fiery halo that made her radiant. The halo was no metaphysical effect; all angels literally glowed in the sun or moon's light, and it was the manifestation of the beauty of their souls. She was a surprisingly beautiful baby, even physically, and she had inherited her mother's blue-black hair that marked the royal bloodline.

After she had been bathed and returned to Alyenna, she was still unhappy. Alyenna had no doubt she knew why. She looked at Talia and smiled. "Fetch Alexander, please." She watched her guardian slip out and then smiled at Malthus as he sat beside her on the bed. "Are you pleased with your heir?"

His fingers trembled as he lightly touched the dark hair on his daughter's head. "Did you have to give me such a beautiful child, Aly? She will be *lethal* at sixteen!"

She bit back a laugh. "She will be well-guarded." She looked at the door as it opened and Alexander peeked around the side. "Alexander. Come meet your princess." She patted the bed with her free hand. "Join me."

He climbed up to sit beside her, and his breath caught as he saw the tiny newborn in her arms. "She's so *small!*"

At barely seven pounds and only thirteen inches long, the baby was indeed exceptionally delicate and tiny. The frame came from her mother as well; Alyenna barely stood at five-four in height, and she was quite slender herself. "Here," she said softly. "Hold out your arms."

He did so, and she put the baby gently into his care. He felt enchanted with the little princess as he looked at her delicate features and soft hair. She was very fussy still, and he softly nuzzled her cheek with his nose. "Hey," he murmured. "It's okay now." He lifted his head as she opened her eyes, and he found himself staring into the iridescent green eyes that marked all Lightlings. These eyes, however, were deeper and more luminous than any he had ever seen.

She stared up at him with something like wonder in her eyes and then she sighed and snuggled against him without a further fuss. In that moment, he fell helplessly and hopelessly in love. "I'll guard you," he whispered. "I promise."

Alyenna leaned her head against Malthus's shoulder and just smiled. In a very soft voice, Malthus murmured, "I concede, Aly. You were right. He *is* perfect." In more ways than one, in fact. He should never have doubted his wife's instincts for their child.

"What is her name?" Alexander asked.

Malthus smiled. "Maitena. It means 'butterfly princess.' We were thinking to call her Mai for short."

"Maitena." He liked it. His little butterfly. He would never let anything hurt her. *Ever.*

Unfortunately, a little pain must always enter into any angel's life, and it inevitably occurred at the age of two when their wings started to break in. It was a painful and often frightening process for the toddler that was far worse than teething. The pain was not just physical but *meta*physical since the wings were technically affixed to the soul and only looked as if they were connected at the back.

The wings grew from the soul outward toward the back where they would break through the skin and unfurl the first time. After that, the angel would be able to keep them out as a physical set of limbs or put them back into their soul where they resided as pure spiritual energy. To touch an angel's wings was to literally touch their soul, and it was the reason why an angel only gave their wings to a destined mate. During Unfurling, as it was known, the baby angel was often unhappy to be held by anyone but a guardian, whose core power could heal an angel as profoundly as it could destroy them.

Eliana and Mai started Unfurling within mere days of each other, and poor Maduin and Alexander had their hands full trying to keep them soothed. They would frequently find themselves pacing and rocking their angels in an effort to keep them from feeling the pain too terribly. It was not helped any by the fact that both girls had mental comprehension on par with a five-year-old human. Angels developed faster than humans, females faster still than males, and royals faster on top of that. They knew what was happening, and it was scary.

Alyenna watched them pacing and winced as she stepped into the grand hall outside the throne room. Behind her, a male voice said dryly, "You would just *have* to have had a Shaman and made us share her misery."

She turned with a grin. "You're just jealous, Anthony."

Anthony Summerwing grinned back at her. "I'm not. I'm really not." He leaned down and kissed her cheek. "Hello, lovely. Where's your idiot husband?"

"It's nice to see you too, Anthony," Malthus complained as he approached. "Get your lips off my wife." He smiled to where Anthony's wife, Gillian, stood. "I still think you're crazy."

Gillian laughed at him. "Or destiny is."

Malthus and Anthony—and Anthony's cousin, Robert—had been friends for more than a decade before Anthony had met Gillian. That meeting had canceled his betrothal to Alyenna. The very next year, at her eighteenth birthday party, she had encountered Malthus and found her own destiny had been nearby and unseen all along. Robert, being younger, had not met his mate until barely a year ago. Mauri had immediately joined the tight circle as if she had always belonged, and all three women shared a mutual exasperation for their husbands' antics. Twelve or twenty-something, they still egged each other on as boys.

Anthony and Alyenna had been best friends since birth and were more like brother and sister than not. There was a year separating their ages just as it did between Anthony and Gillian's son, Joshua, and Mai. The Summerwing family ruled the Crystal Kingdom the way the Everbird family ruled the Chalice Kingdom. They visited each other as frequently as could be managed, though this was the first get-together in several months.

It was for that reason that Alyenna spotted the delicate brunette slowly approaching and hastily rushed over to help. "Mauri! Oh my." She bit her lip as she helped her surrogate cousin-in-law sit down. In each of Marui's arms was a tiny, brown haired baby. "Twins." She looked up as Robert walked in. "Because of course you would just have to prove that angels *can* have twins after all." It was unheard of, to be sure.

Robert Sheridan grinned at her. "Well, you can't wholly blame me! I blame Mauri's one-quarter human blood." He smoothed a tender hand down his wife's hair. "They're fraternal twins. The elder, Laila, is to be a Warrior. The younger, Kev, is to be a Wizard. He is already brimming with magic where his older sister has none."

"I wish I'd had just one Shaman," Mauri groused.

"No," Alyenna and Malthus protested hastily, "you don't!"

It made the entire Summerwing family start laughing. Perched in Gillian's arms, the fair-haired three-year-old prince looked at his family with a bit of confusion and then looked up at his mother. He shared a five-year-old's comprehension with the two princesses though he was a year older. "Why is it funny?" he asked.

She nuzzled his white hair, inherited from his father. The two royal bloodlines were nearly opposites in many ways, with one carrying black hair and the other carrying white. The colors were unusual among angels of all ilks, thus setting them apart more. "You'll know when you're a bit older, my love." She winced as she heard the crying briefly gain in force. "However, I am grateful you are now past that."

Her son also winced a bit as he realized that his best friends were now going through what he had gone through the year before. Malthus admitted, "We have been grateful for Alexander and Maduin. I don't know how you managed without a guardian for Josh."

"Sheer dumb luck. But, speaking of guardians." Robert turned toward the door and called, "Sami!" When the slim young girl had walked inside, he companionably put a hand on her shoulder. "Meet Sami Dumont. She is just ten years old, and she is already partly trained as a guardian. She will be the twins' guardian specifically and also serves now as one for Josh unless and until we find him his own." He eyed his cousin. "You know, I'm a bit suspicious of that one servant boy in the kitchens. Kayden is his name, right?"

"Kayden Tartino," Mauri confirmed.

Josh promptly brightened. "Kayden can be my guardian?"

The adults exchanged a look and then smiled wryly. If Josh was that happy with the idea, then it was likely Kayden was indeed a guardian even if he himself did not know it. It did happen sometimes. Guardians without magic could be easily overlooked. "We'll turn him and Sami likewise over to Alexander for training if you don't mind," Anthony told Alyenna. "He is by *far* the best we've ever seen, and I don't mean merely for his age. Our guardians jokingly say they wish they could hand us over."

Alyenna grinned. "He is gifted, to be sure." She smiled at Sami. "Hello, Sami. I'm Alyenna. I'm very honored to meet you. This is my husband, Malthus."

Sami smiled at her. At ten, she was already

quite beautiful, and her striking emerald hair and eyes made her stand out in a crowd. Truthfully, ninety percent of humans shared gender-transcending beauty with angels to some degree or another. Most blamed the magic and did not mind at all. "I am pleased to meet you as well." She frowned toward the throne room as she heard more crying. "They are not happy."

Mauri smiled at her. "Uh-oh. I hear the healer's instinct stirring." To the others, she said, "Sami is an Air element with great healing magic."

"Ah!" Malthus gestured to the throne room. "Feel free to offer your help. I am sure Alexander and Maduin will not mind."

Sami hesitated and then sighed and went into the throne room. Her need to heal was always getting her into trouble. Babies, especially baby angels, unnerved her more than a little. Josh had terrified her when she had first joined the royal household the year before, and she still wasn't sure how to handle her newborn angels. Her nerves weren't aided any when she saw the two boys pacing a bit frantically with very fussy and very upset little angels in their arms. "Uhm. Can I help?"

Alexander glanced at her, recognized a fellow guardian as well as a healer, and immediately walked over to plop Mai into her arms. "Make her smile."

Sami boggled at the princess, and Mai stared back with wide-eyed consternation as if she had no idea who this new person was or why she was there. Perhaps miraculously, she stopped crying entirely. To Sami's dismay, she was promptly handed the other princess as well. Eliana also blinked at her and stopped crying. She found herself being pinned under matching iridescent fascination and looked at her fellow guardians helplessly. "I've just met you and already I hate you."

Alexander and Maduin sat down hard on the floor. "You're the answer to our prayers," the latter complained. "*Ugh.*" He fell over on his back. "Remind me to write to my parents and apologize profusely for what I put them through when I was Unfurling. I have a whole new respect for my own species!"

Alexander smiled at Sami wryly. "I'm Alexander Solomon. This is Maduin Grimoire."

"Sami Dumont." She blinked as both little girls leaned in and actually sniffed at her. "Er, what are they doing?"

Maduin sat up and grinned. "For one, they smell your magic. For another, they're checking to see if you have any angelic blood. You don't, but they're checking anyway. That's how we can identify each other. Every angel has a unique scent that moves through the family tree. You humans match DNA. We match scents."

The girls were still staring at Sami. "They are really starting to unnerve me."

"You get used to it," Alexander offered. "An angel's gaze can be very piercing, especially when they are powerful. You've got the two most powerful female angels alive in your arms." He got back up to his feet. "I guess I've got a lot to teach you." He smiled. "How old are you?"

"Ten."

"Fourteen." He jerked a thumb at Maduin. "Nine.

Sami stared. She would have thought Alexander closer to seventeen. He was much more mature in a way more typical of angels. "I guess I don't mind." She winced and quickly held the girls closer as they suddenly began to cry again. "Uh-oh. Your rest is over, guys." From where she had a hand on each of their backs, she could feel a sudden surge of power under their skin. "Something's moving."

Maduin scrambled up and quickly took Eliana, and Alexander took Mai. Mai curled against her guardian and whimpered in pain. "Alex! It hurts! Make it stop! You make it better!"

"Angel." He buried his face in her hair. "Just hang on. It won't be much longer." It had been a week. He would lose his mind if she suffered much more.

Eliana's wings blessedly broke through the following day. The minute Maduin saw the black feathers emerging from her skin, he was able to call in Sami. The healer nearly balked when she found out what she had to do, but she swallowed her nerves and gave in. Quite simply, the safest way to spare an angel unnecessary damage both internal and external was to gently cut the skin of their back to loosen pressure and let nature take over.

Her hands were steady enough to cut Eliana's skin, and the angel's wings promptly broke out with enough force to make the walls briefly shake. The cuts could then be healed, and her wings drooped as exhaustion claimed her. Maduin let out the breath he had been holding and rocked her as she slept, finally, peacefully in his arms. "She'll be able to go through Awakening at five without any trouble now."

Awakening was when an angel *truly* became one. They would manifest their power more wholly and take command of either their fire or lightning, and if they had magic, they would start to use it. It would continue to develop until final maturity at eighteen where it would hit peak and cement. Awakening was relatively safe, if slightly traumatic, in children. If an angel somehow went without Awakening until eighteen or later, it

S.J. GARRETT

could be deadly to them and the people around them.

Sami looked at the tiny black wings on Eliana's back and smiled. "I never realized how cute a baby angel's wings can be."

"You won't say that when your twins start flying and you can't catch 'em."

She winced. "Please don't remind me. I'm already panicking."

The door suddenly opened sharply, and a maid said urgently, "Sami, please hurry. Alexander is calling for you. Princess Maitena's wings are breaking through and she's in *agony*."

Sami scrambled out the door and rushed through the palace to the princess' bedroom. The instant she opened the door, she realized why there was such a panic. The very walls were vibrating in the force of Mai's cries, and her power was making the air quiver violently. Sami could *see* the waves. "Oh my god."

"Sami, hurry!" Alexander snapped. "She's going to tear something!"

She ran over and grabbed the silver dagger Alexander wore on his hip. It was the mark of his role as Mai's guardian, and it was only fitting it be used to end her Unfurling. As Sami was about to cut her skin, however, she realized in shock that the feathers poking through the angel's skin were neither white nor black. They were gray. "What the hell?"

"Sami!"

She shook her head and then swiftly made the small incisions needed. Mai's wings almost literally exploded through the openings, and they did it hard enough that the power knocked Sami flat on the ground. Paintings fell off the walls, and the floor cracked in several places. Eerie silence descended as Mai slumped over against Alexander's shoulder and stopped crying. The shimmering gray wings on her back unfurled slowly and then folded once more as she finally fell asleep, exhausted from the soul out.

Sami carefully got to her feet. "Unbelievable," she murmured. She lightly touched Mai's power with hers and felt, clearly, the Shadow element inside the angel. "Shadow." She looked at her friend and saw the way he had his eyes closed as he rocked Mai. She just smiled. "Alex, did you know they were gray?"

"I was wondering," he admitted. "Whenever her wings moved, gray power moved in her eyes. The only gray elemental power is Shadow. She always had both light and dark inside her." He rubbed his cheek over Mai's hair. "I don't know how much more she could have taken." He looked at the room in consternation. "Her parents are going to kill us."

They were more relieved with their

daughter's ended Unfurling than they were vexed by the need to do repairs. They had her bed moved into their room until they were done, but she was having none of that. She waited until her parents were asleep before sneaking out of her bed, creeping through the palace, and tiptoeing into Alexander's room. He would always let her snuggle into bed beside him, and his heartbeat let her sleep peacefully without the sanctuary of her room.

No one really could figure out what her Shadow element or gray wings meant. The most adept historians and scientists just threw their hands in the air and decided to wait. If it was related to the Shadow Elemine, then there was no knowing what it would all mean. Life would just have to go on until they found their answers.

Whatever they may be.

2
Shadow of the Moon

Life indeed went on. Josh went through Awakening at five and immediately began Warrior training. His twin cousins, then two, went through the painful Unfurling process. Poor Sami had her hands full, to be sure, and she heavily relied on Kayden's help to handle both her angels. The year following, Mai and Eliana went through Awakening as well. Eliana started Wizard training, and Mai began training in both thanks to being a Shaman.

Proving yet again to be unusual, Mai developed both fire and lighting that blended together into the rare force known as Firai. It was as legendary as the Shadow Elemine itself. White fire and black lightning had blended to create an exceptionally potent force. Only one such as Mai, perfectly balanced between Light and Dark, could have ever used it. Yet, the Firai turned out to be just one of her new 'gifts.'

Malthus had taken her out to the gardens for some fresh air, and he glanced away for only one moment. It was a moment long enough for Mai to wander off on her own, and she crawled through a hole in the fence to get outside the castle grounds. She was still very tiny for her age and she fit through places even her cousin could not.

She had made it only a few feet beyond the wall before one of the local monsters found her. Instinct made her run away, but it chased her quickly. She found herself cornered against a wall, and she squeezed her eyes shut as the monster lunged for her. When it suddenly yelped, her eyes flew wide. A familiar figure was crouched in front of her, and Moon magic swirled around the sword he held. "Alex!" She grabbed the back of his tunic and held on with all her strength.

"I am going to tan your hide!" her guardian muttered. "I about had a heart attack when I felt you leave the grounds!"

She had never, ever been able to get away with anything or hide anything from her guardian. He always knew where she was and what she was doing, and she thought he either had spies or could read her mind. She didn't mind at all. She was happiest with him there. He was her favoritest person ever, more than even Josh and Eliana.

The monster lunged in again, and Alexander swung his arm up to block. Fangs sank deep into his arm, and blood welled. Molten fury ripped through Mai that the person she loved most had been hurt. "Let. GO!" Her small hands lifted, and a blast of Firai streaked from her palms. It not only blew the beast into bits, it also knocked her over onto her bottom in the process. "Owie!"

Alexander just sighed. As protective of his princess as he was, she was truly just as bad about him. He started to turn to help her, and too late he heard the snarling that was more danger. Another beast leapt out of the trees and slammed into him hard enough to knock him flat. He cursed viciously as he struggled to keep jaws from closing on his neck.

Another monster emerged and started toward Mai. Alexander's heart stopped for a moment and then determination filled him as he reached for all of his magic. His angel's life was worth more than his. Just before he could release the spell, something entirely different snarled viciously and tore out of the trees. The large gray wolf ripped the beast away from Mai and sent it running with a pained yip. The wolf then rushed over and snapped at the neck of the beast fighting Alexander. It also backed up sharply and then ran off.

Alexander painfully sat up and winced as more than one wound winced. In addition to the first bite, he had gotten clawed and bitten a few more times. Mai flung herself at him and wound her arms around his neck. "I'm sorry!" she wailed against his shoulder. "Don't die, Alex! You can't die! You can't leave me!"

"Butterfly." He smoothed his hand over her back gently. "I'm not dead. I'm not even close to it. Your friend helped me." He smiled over her head at the wolf. He knew a sentient creature when he saw it. "Thank you." He gingerly got to his feet and then bent and put Mai on the wolf's back. She was just small enough to ride. "There you go."

She leaned down and hugged the wolf around the neck and nuzzled his fur. The wolf rubbed his head against hers, and she sat up. "Tynan! He's Tynan!" She smiled up at Alexander. "Can I keep him? Please? Please? He belongs with me."

"If your parents don't object. And that's also pending your parents not grounding you until you're eighteen."

When Malthus spotted his little girl riding

on the wolf's back, he could only groan. "Damn it, Maitena! I am too young to have a heart attack!" At twenty-eight, it was a legitimate concern. He picked up his daughter and settled her on his hip before eyeing the rather ragged guardian with her. "You're a mess, kid."

Alexander grimaced. "I can imagine I am. I better get my wounds cleaned up. By the way, you have a new pet."

"Wait, what?"

"Alex!" Mai threw herself forward, and Alexander hastily caught her before Malthus dropped her. "Come on, Tynan!" she said cheerfully. "You can sleep on my bed! An' we can get you a collar!"

Malthus blinked as he watched the wolf trot behind Alexander and Mai. On a sigh, he said, "Aly, your child will be the death of me yet."

Alexander was halfway toward his room when one of the ladies-in-waiting ran into him in the hall. She stared for a moment and then winced when she saw the blood on his tunic and the wounds visible beneath the tears. "Oh, my. Our Mai does keep you guessing." She smiled and tilted her head flirtatiously as she looked up at him from under her lashes. "I have healing magic. I would be happy to help you."

A familiar stormy look settled over Mai's face that meant her temper was on the rise.

Alexander just smiled. "I thank you for your offer, but I can handle this. It's not very much. If anything, perhaps Mai can practice her healing magic." He continued down the hall with barely a pause.

Mai looked back over his shoulder and stuck her tongue out at the courtier. The young woman blinked and then hastily swallowed a laugh as she hurried away. Truthfully, the entire kingdom had noticed that the princess was *very* possessive of her guardian, and vice-versa. It went far, far beyond the normal bond of a guardian and angel and did, in fact, smack of a budding bond between destined mates. It would certainly be interesting to see what happened when she hit final maturity.

It got interesting much sooner than that. If there was any one moment most angels dreaded in their evolution, other than Unfurling, it was the time known as a Flare that they entered into when they were sixteen. It was so named since it was referred to as the first flare of final maturity. Like the match that flared when first lit, an angel's appeal went into hyper-drive so dramatically that they almost literally started to ooze sexuality. The only people ever spared from attraction to a Flaring angel were their own parents or anyone too young to feel any sort of desire.

Josh entered his Flare the year before Mai and Eliana. He proved to be more of a problem than anticipated, enough so that Kayden found himself calling upon Sami, Alexander, and Maduin alike to help keep the prince from getting a broken heart. The real problem with Flaring angels was that they were most times vulnerable to their own power. It could only be tempered by an angel finding a single target and effectively focusing all their desire on them. It was a strange and wonderful and terrifying time for the angel as much as it was for anyone else. You couldn't take anything they said or did seriously.

His Flare ended a month before Eliana's began. She Flared a bit brighter than anticipated, and Maduin found himself literally having to physically beat back some suitors. She took it with the same good humor she took the rest of life, and she didn't at all mind spending more time with her guardian. She had known for all of her life that he was the one she loved most. Final maturity would merely be a confirmation of what her wings and heart had told her all along.

She kept it mum, though. She was, after all, sixteen. He wouldn't believe her. He'd had enough trouble with his own sixteenth year. Rather than deal with the complications of being a guardian *and* Flaring, he had effectively locked himself inside his room at the castle for the entire year, and his sympathetic angel had kept him company. By not exposing himself to anyone old enough to either feel or cause desire, he had weathered the normally tumultuous storm. Eliana, now old enough for both, knew that her Flare would test them both. But, when it ended and the desire between them only got worse, he would see what she had all along. She was fairly sure he already knew, but his was a cautious soul. It was why he was able to keep her healthy. She liked charging in.

For all the problems Flare could bring, it was genuinely a time to be celebrated, particularly when it came to the heirs to the thrones. They flared brightest, longest, and would continue to burn the most thanks to being the most powerful. A ball was planned for the night of Mai's sixteenth birthday, and she found that she herself actually was looking forward to it. Tradition dictated that the first dance belonged to the heir's guardian. She had been looking forward to dancing with Alexander all of her life.

She woke the morning of her birthday and braced her shoulders before looking into a mirror. Her reflection greeted her, and she winced. She could see her halo even just standing in her lamplight, and that meant that she was not just Flaring, she was *FLARING*. Angels couldn't normally see their own halos unless in Flare, and even then, still only in the sun or moonlight. It almost seemed as if she was going to glow unless she was in absolute darkness—and that was not yet a certainty anyway. She groaned and dropped her head into her hands. It was going to be twelve months of hell.

Her door cracked open, and Eliana peeked in. She promptly winced. "Oof! Okay, yeah, you're *bad*." She walked over to her cousin and sighed. "Things would be so much easier if you weren't gorgeous and sexy to start with."

Ever since puberty had kicked in, Mai had begun exuding an aura of sheer sultry sensuality that was normally reserved for just the age of sixteen. She didn't just transcend gender; she seemed to transcend beauty itself. Added to that was a hauntingly gorgeous face, long blue-black hair, bright iridescent green eyes, and a body that, while not curvy, was somehow the perfect ideal of desire.

She was still tiny, though. She wasn't technically short at five-four, but she was so utterly delicate that she seemed impossibly smaller. Eliana stood a few inches taller, many pounds heavier, and she had the curves that Mai had always wistfully wished to have herself.

The cousins were near opposites in most ways, perhaps fitting to their opposite races. Eliana had pale pink hair and iridescent red eyes, the latter of which marked all pureblood Darklings. Yet, despite her own beauty, she had merely been mildly attractive from the onset of puberty, just enough to make people look at her with the start of potential desire. She had only started to ooze sexuality with the start of her Flare. She was relatively normal for a royal angel overall.

"You can't stay in here all year," she noted reasonably.

Mai winced. "You're picking up Alex's habit of reading my mind."

"No, I read your face." She shoved her cousin at the large closet taking up one side of the tower. "Dress to feel good about yourself, however much you think that may make it be worse. Let's be honest: it's not only your face or body, it's your soul and halo. You could go out in a gunny sack, Alexander's cloak, and a hood, and you'd still have people following you with their tongues lolling."

Tynan, lying on the end of Mai's bed, made a sound suspiciously like a snort of laughter. Both females ignored him. Mai grumbled a little more, mostly for form, and then went into her closet. Dressing to feel good meant her favorite gray dress and black bodice with its fat white ribbons. It meant leaving her hair down so it hung to her hips and then putting on the silver coronet that marked her as the crown princess. She felt happy enough with how she looked, but that didn't mean she was looking forward to the coming months.

Eliana left her to pull her shoes on and headed down out of the tower that Mai now called home; she had moved into the tower bedroom on her thirteenth birthday, as was the right of a princess. Eliana had a different tower all her own. She found Alexander at the bottom of the stairs and told him gravely, "You're going to need the other guardians. You may also need Josh and the entire royal guard."

He just sighed. "I had assumed, Eliana. Scoot." He gave her a little pat on the back. "Maduin is waiting to take you out for breakfast and to buy Mai's birthday gift."

"'kay!" She hurried down the hall happily.

He leaned against the wall and waited, only a tiny hint of tension to his shoulders belying that he knew his life was about to be more complicated. When his angel very carefully opened the door at the bottom and peeked out, he almost choked. He had already been carefully controlling and concealing an attraction to her that had started as a minor thing but had grown more and more powerful as she aged. The way his hunger for her leapt in that moment, he knew that the coming year would be as difficult for him as for her—if not more.

The truth was there staring him in the face. He did not merely love his princess, he was nearly wholly sure that he was *in love* with his princess. Only final maturity would say for sure whether he was her destined mate as he believed, or if he merely had an unrequited love that was not too terribly uncommon where angels were concerned. He would accept whichever direction it went, and continue to be happy so long as she smiled at him.

She did smile now when she saw him, but it was hesitant and fleeting. Nerves filled her green eyes as she slowly stepped into the hall. "Alex . . ."

"Of course I'm attracted to you," he told her reasonably. "Maitena, at this point, the stone statues in the grand hall may leave their posts in an effort to follow you. I'm twenty-eight, not eight, and you are in Flare. You're also gorgeous, and I love you to start with. I'm fair game for nature's idea of a practical joke on angels and the people around them alike. I was also prepared for this because of Josh and Eliana. Now come here and get the hug you want."

Her smile spread and reached her eyes. He always knew the right thing to tell her. She rushed across the hall and threw her arms around him fiercely. He was her everything. Her guardian, her best friend, and her hero. She loved no one more. Truthfully, she held more than a little suspicion that he might be her destined mate. Over the last two years, she had been noticing more and more just how *ridiculously* gorgeous he was, until it was a wonder she could even keep her emotions under wraps. If he wasn't her mate, then she had a hell of a case of the hots for her guardian. Which, then again, was not unusual at sixteen. A lot of angels often turned to their guardian as a target to weather the storm.

Her day got worse before it got better. She was in the grand ballroom organizing the decorations for her party when Talia came to find her. Mai eyed the guardian's visible reluctance and then winced. "Uh-oh. Why won't I like this?"

"Your mother sent me to get you, honey." Talia put an arm around Mai's shoulders and herded her toward the grand entrance hall. "Brace yourself," she muttered.

Mai groaned softly as she saw the line outside the castle doors. It was at least fifty bodies deep of all genders and races, and they were vying for a chance to look in the windows at her. "Let me go hide," she pleaded with her parents. "Please. Have mercy for your loving child."

"Maitena." Alyenna pulled her over and firmly pushed her forward where she could be seen by the people outside. "Just get it over with. The sooner they see you, the sooner they can get back to their business. You know everyone has been anticipating this."

The mob scene didn't start to dissipate. It actually started getting worse as more and more people began crowding in. The interior guards had to hastily jump forward and bar the doors even more before they opened. The heavy, thick wooden doors still began to look strained. Talia looked at Alyenna and said only, "And I thought *you* were bad."

Mai gulped and whirled around to run away. She ran right into Alexander where he had silently come up behind her. She immediately ducked under his cloak and hid behind his back. "Make them go away!" came her despairing wail. "I don't want to be Ceres' sex symbol!"

Talia bit her lip, hard, before she started laughing. Even Malthus and Alyenna were hard-pressed to keep a straight face. "Take her away, Alexander," Alyenna murmured. "I suppose we shall have to play by ear. Our Mai just never does anything the easy way."

"Love you, too, Mother," came the answering mutter.

By the time evening arrived and the ball was in its starting stages, Mai had ensconced herself in her room and not emerged. Her ladies-in-waiting arrived to help her dress and discovered they were not immune to her appeal. They loved her enough to not want her to be uncomfortable, so they immediately fetched Alyenna and Eliana to help Mai instead. If this was going to be the pattern of the year, it was going to be vexing for all involved.

Alexander was in his room getting dressed in his formal uniform when someone knocked on the door. "Enter," he called. When he saw Sami walk in, he grinned. "Hey, Sami. You look a little more comfortable in that uniform than the last time I saw you."

"Practice makes perfect," Sami retorted. "Josh's ball at the least prepared me." She winced. "I understand that his Flare in no way prepared anyone for Mai however." All guardians, as close to the kingdoms as they were, were allowed the informality of using nicknames and not titles with the royal families. In many ways, guardians were considered part of the royal families. They held unofficial titles of nobility themselves.

"Not even Eliana prepared us," he confirmed. "She's *bad*, Sami."

She studied him for a few moments and then smiled. "Alex," she asked her best friend politely, "does someone have something of a crush on his princess even without her Flare?"

"I'm not going to answer a question with an

obvious answer." He yanked at his cuffs. "I have no idea if I'm her mate or if I'm just dealing with a relatively normal unrequited love for an angel. It happens, unfortunately, and guardians are more prone to it than others."

"Fair enough." She leaned against a table. "Well, allow me to at least put your mind at ease about one thing: the betrothal between Mai and Josh will no doubt be called off within a few short years. Perhaps four, to be exact."

He lifted a brow. "Four years?"

"When the twins hit maturity. Josh and Laila are, hmm, *possessive* of each other, shall we say?"

He grinned. "I had begun to wonder about that. Well, they're only second cousins, and the choice of destined mates is never predictable. I got suspicious a year ago, really. Poor Laila had just started puberty when Josh entered Flare. She was affected by it significantly more than Kev." His grin turned a bit wicked. "Speaking of Kev, has Kayden yet admitted he's a bit more possessive and protective of Kev than you are?"

She snorted. "He's getting there. He's just being very careful for obvious reasons. I, however, find nothing sacred. I already spoke to Robert and Mauri. If Kayden is Kev's destined mate, and Laila is Josh's, then I will hand guardianship of Kev over to Kayden and we'll share Laila." She smiled. "Unless I happen to find another angel to guard. On a related note—and no, I'm not subtle—is Mai's other cousin going to be here?"

"Aya?" He snorted. "No, you're not subtle, and yes, she is."

Aya Revelry was Mai and Eliana's second cousin, connected through Alyenna's aunt. She had more human blood than angelic blood—she was only an eighth Lightling—but her angelic blood was royal and therefore made her more like a half-breed. She also had the Shaman gift, and it had come with the gift of Sight as well. She was a year younger than Mai and Eliana, and just angelic enough to be already catching eyes. Lucky for her, she would not go through Flare. And at least where Sami was concerned, she certainly didn't need to!

"I could just be drawn to her as a guardian. I might also be overly possessive and protective because her Sight often makes her vulnerable." Sami smiled. "I suppose we shall have to see what happens as she gets older. They say an angel is always worth waiting for."

"You're *really* not subtle."

The ball was attended by hundreds of people. Maduin stayed at Eliana's side the entire time, and Alexander did not leave Mai. Flaring angels were not allowed to be unchaperoned. They either needed to be with a guardian or a parent. In the princesses' case, the only acceptable other alternative was Josh. When he walked up to where they stood, he said solemnly, "When I say you have my sympathies, you know I mean it." Even without Flare, he made a devastating figure in the white dress uniform of a royal angel. Many wistful eyes had been fixed to him the entire time.

Mai looked positively lethal in her white ball gown, and those who looked at her could nearly not look away again. Her hair had been pinned up with a few loose ringlets, and she by far looked more like an adult than a sixteen-year-old. She had looked sixteen at the age of thirteen. It was why Alexander had never felt uncomfortable with his desire for her, or why Sami was not bothered to be attracted to Aya. Accelerated angelic maturity applied both mentally and physically. It was very common that angels who had destined mates in humans could find age gaps of anywhere from five to fifteen years between them.

Josh leaned down and kissed Mai's cheek. "I get your second dance," he told her.

She grinned. "You want to make Laila jealous." He just winked and ambled away, and she looked at the others gravely. "At least Laila will have her revenge when she hits Flare." She winced as understanding hit. "Oof. Her and Kev.

Same time. Yikes. So not fair."

"No," Maduin said dryly, "not fair would be you two, Josh, and the twins all being the same age."

Alexander grimaced. "Thank you for that nightmare, Maduin. I didn't need to sleep tonight." He glanced up as he heard trumpets and then looked down at Mai. He skimmed his finger over her cheek. "I will see you in a few moments for our dance."

She smiled up at him almost shyly. "Okay." She saw the floor beginning to clear as the trumpets continued to play, and she slowly walked out into the middle of the floor.

Everyone began to cheer, and the majority of the crowd also sighed happily. "Ladies and gentlemen," Talia said clearly. As the eldest guardian of the two kingdoms, she was considered the High Guardian and therefore given the duty to announce the royal heirs. "Her Royal Highness, the crown princess and heir to the throne of the Chalice Kingdom, Maitena Everbird. Her Flare has begun. In two years, she will be an adult and we will celebrate again." The cheers picked up again, and she smiled as she continued, "As is tradition, the princess' first dance belongs to her guardian, Alexander Solomon."

Alexander walked quietly across the floor to

where Mai stood, and more sighing was done. He was by far as beautiful as any angel, and his utter devotion to his princess was almost as sexy as his strong guardian body. He brought her hand to his lips as he bowed, and she sank into a graceful curtsey. Music spilled into the air as he drew her into his arms and began to lead her across the floor.

Standing along the side of the room, Josh observed the dance and then murmured to Kayden, "Call me crazy, but you sure as hell didn't look at me like that when you danced with me."

Kayden just snorted softly. Sami wasn't the only one who had been prodding Alexander about his emotions for Mai. All of the guardians had said something at one time or another. His eyes drifted to where Kev stood with his parents, and he bit back a wistful sigh. An angel was *well* worth waiting for. At twenty-eight, he was a few months younger than Alexander and fourteen years older than Kev. He didn't mind. Destined mates knew no barrier. An angel's mate was what they needed. If an angel needed a mate that much older, then they would have one. He glanced at the floor and smiled. Sometimes stronger angels needed it more than most.

Mai, being a Shaman, channeled magic through music. Her body became an instrument that moved with a grace as magical as it was beautiful. Alexander matched her perfectly, and he handled her smaller frame with a gentleness that was nearly intimate. The soft flush to her face and the adoration in her eyes as she looked up at him only increased her appeal more. The look in his eyes spoke just as many volumes.

Bets had been laid by the end of the dance. Not a single person there doubted that the princess and her guardian were destined mates. The question was whether or not they would figure it out on her eighteenth birthday, or before.

Josh indeed got Mai's second dance—his right as her betrothed—and he was quite happy to see the stormy look of temper on Laila's face. Mai just laughed at him. She danced with Eliana as well, and Aya and Kev. She also danced with her father, and when he swung her in the air as if she was five again, her laughter rang out to make everyone smile. She was the greatest treasure of the kingdom. She brought joy to the very air around her.

She danced with others as well, though only the ones she could trust to not get fresh. Namely, those either too young or already mated. As Malthus saw her dancing with a gray-haired young man, he asked, "Who is that? I've never seen him before and yet he looks familiar."

Alyenna and Anthony looked as well, and both knew how he felt. Eliana said nothing. She had her suspicions but she wasn't going to blab them. It was up to Mai to clue everyone in, if she wanted.

By the time the halfway mark of Mai's sixteenth year approached, she was nearly at her wits' end. She couldn't leave the palace without fear of being accosted, even if she was never alone when she went out. People were blinded by her sensuality, and that meant Alexander and even Maduin had found themselves dealing out more than one black eye in her defense. She had dealt a few as well, unfortunately.

The only people she could handle being around for extended periods of time were her parents, Eliana, and Alexander. Not even Josh could really handle it without things getting uncomfortable on both sides. For the betrothed pair, it left them feeling as if a brother was attracted to his sister—another clue that the betrothal simply would not work. They were obligated to hold the betrothal until one or the other of them hit final maturity and confirmed their destined mate, but they were ready to call it off right then and there. No one could blame them; most everyone in both kingdoms knew who the heirs were destined to love.

Talia watched from a window as Alexander and Mai walked in the gardens together and said absently to Alyenna, "Spring or fall?"

"Fall, of course." Alyenna continued work on the dress she was mending. "Royal weddings are always much nicer in fall."

Another botched attempt to merely go into town to get flowers had Mai hiding herself in her tower. Eliana came up to join her and flopped down on the bed beside her cousin. "What's really eating you, hon?" she asked. "And don't tell me it's nothing. I know you best other than Alexander. You are far more bothered by this than I would have expected. What's going on?"

Mai sighed and pulled the pillow off her face. "It's silly."

"I promise not to laugh."

"I was *this* close to having the worst first kiss experience ever." She scowled. "Some jerk tried to plant one on me before Alex could get her away, and it spooked me. I don't want my first kiss to be the worst memory of my life! Is that petty of me in the scale of things?"

Eliana stared at her. "That is an entirely legitimate concern, and oh my god, I would be spooked too!" She huffed out a breath. "I took care of that problem for myself right after my birthday. I planted one on Maduin."

.J. GARRETT

"Is that why he was glowering at you for the rest of the day?"

"I knocked his socks off, and he's trying so very hard to be noble and not 'take advantage' of my Flare. Never mind that the only reason he's succeeding is because I am choosing to be patient. It's tempting though. Really, really, *really* tempting."

Mai snorted softly as she sat up, and then she sighed again. "Honestly, I'm not asking to get my socks knocked off, as appealing as that sounds. I just want it to be nice. Something I can remember later fondly. A bright spot in this year of hell."

"How about me?" Eliana offered. "I'm relatively unaffected by you—and I still say we're magnetically canceling each other out—so, why not? Give us both a good memory." She grinned. "And let's face it. Another toss of the dice and we'd probably be destined mates."

"'Tis true!" Mai had also known that for years. The force and fury of their love for each other had more than once perplexed outsiders. "Or twins. We could've gone either way." She scooted closer. "Alright. You may proceed to at the least make my socks slightly wiggle. They don't need to leave my feet for me to be happy."

"I love you. Just saying that again." Eliana caught her chin and leaned in with the intent of

6

kissing her, but just before their lips touched, they both broke down in a giggling fit. "This is *not* going to work!" she managed to say. "Apparently, I'm not even affected enough to just kiss you!"

"Argh! That is just not fair!" Mai fell over on her back again. A clock rang in the distance, and she said, "Don't you have a luncheon with Maduin?"

"Speak of the devil! I do indeed." She leaned over and kissed Mai's forehead. "You'll figure something out." She headed out of the tower, and she shut the door behind her.

As soon as it was closed, the wolf lying near the fireplace said, "I'd offer myself, but I would have the same problem. I'm afraid I'm somewhere between Josh and Eliana, where I am not really attracted to you, but I also feel slightly awkward at the very idea."

Mai snorted as she sat up. "I appreciate the offer regardless, Tynan." She rubbed her hands over her eyes. "Is it impractical of me as an angel to wish to get through this unscathed?"

"Not so much impractical as unlikely." He lifted his head to look at her. "Though I do have to say I've been surprised by how well you're weathering this without a target. Eliana has been able to focus all her desire on Maduin, and he's taking it well in stride—socks notwithstanding.

Josh about gave the guardians gray hair. I think if Laila hadn't started puberty partway through, it might have gotten far worse because he would have broken his heart rather than just bruise it. Chasing her as a target kept him somewhat sane, as well as entertained the rest of us. You, on the other hand, the one who is literally a walking embodiment of desire, are all but stunted."

She frowned. "You suppose the two are linked? Maybe I'm leaking out everything I should have inside."

He had to laugh. "It would be just like you to be that contrary."

She briefly stuck her tongue out at him. Having him in her life was like having another brother. At least she wasn't betrothed to this one. "I'm serious."

"So am I. As for your current problem, I think the answer is closer than you think. Alexander."

She blinked. "Alex." She brightened as it dawned on her. "Of course! He already admitted he was attracted to me, and I've definitely been attracted to him since even before this stupid Flare, so there shouldn't be any problem like with Eliana, or you or Josh. And, well, he's Alex. My guardian." Her voice was simple. "I don't trust anyone more than I trust him." She hopped to her feet. "Thanks, Tynan."

He watched her run out of the tower and smiled to himself. "Indeed." He put his head down again and added under his breath, "I hope she glued on her socks this morning."

Mai was an intelligent young woman who had no need to make things potentially awkward. She stopped by the drawing room where her parents were playing cards with Talia and announced, "I'm going to go kiss Alex."

Malthus choked on his water, and Talia patted him helpfully on the back. Alyenna just smiled. "Of course, dear. Ignore your father. He's been enjoying the fact that you've made it easy to keep your heart from being broken. It's such an oddity, and we both appreciate it."

Malthus glowered at her and then sighed at Mai. "You just caught me by surprise. Of course you have my blessing, sweetheart." He smiled ruefully in memory. "My sixteenth year was fairly eventful as well."

Alyenna murmured, "I've heard the stories from Anthony."

"Ignore him. He has a big mouth."

Mai rolled her eyes, and Alyenna laughed, "Maitena, you have our blessings to experiment to whatever degree you so wish, particularly if you are picking a very safe target such as Alexander. We trust him with your very *life* let alone your heart. Sixteen is as lethal on an angel as it is on others, darling. Enjoy it."

Mai immediately whirled and hurried down the hall. She knew she would find her guardian in the library. If he wasn't with her, he was in there writing down more of the stories bouncing around inside his head. He wrote beautiful, fantastical tales that she covetously guarded copies of in her room.

He was indeed in the library, and he was sitting at a desk with pen and paper. Her pulse happily fluttered all over the place as something hot and needy clenched inside. He wore glasses for reading, or writing, and they did delicious things to his face. With every passing day, she found more and more about him that was just too damn attractive for her sanity. Her problem, whatever it was, was absolutely not that her sexuality was all external. At least not for *him*.

Without looking up, he said, "I know you're there, butterfly."

The nickname, as always, fluttered her heart. She linked her hands together as she walked over to him. "Alex?"

The hesitant note had him looking up quickly. He frowned and removed his glasses as he stood. He came around the side of the desk and cupped her cheek. "What's wrong, angel? Why are you so nervous? Is there something wrong?"

"No, not really." She blew out a breath. "I want you to be my first kiss."

He paused. He didn't ask why she was asking him; he knew more about her Flare issues than she probably did, and what he didn't guess, Eliana cheerfully blabbed. He also didn't ask if she was sure. She never did anything unless she was sure. His only hesitation was because she trusted him more than he trusted himself. You couldn't take an angel seriously at sixteen, but she was not a normal angel. "Angel."

Her gaze dropped. "Please? I just . . . want it to be my choice. Something I will remember happily. With someone I love. That loves me."

Whether it was the elusive 'in love' he hoped it was for both of them or merely normal love, there was indeed love between them. He could not deny her when she asked him for something. She asked for so little. She gave instead. She gave unconditionally of love and trust. She looked at him as if he was her hero. How could he deny her? "Come here, butterfly."

She moved closer until he could wrap an arm around her waist. Her heart was already beating hard. He felt so wonderfully warm and hard and secure. Safe. She never felt safer than when he was near. "Alexander."

"Do you want to kiss me, or should I kiss you?" He rubbed his thumb over her full lower lip. She had a mouth designed for kissing. "Gentle or hard? I'm yours to command."

"You kiss me." She smiled. "I think you're probably more experienced. I'll just learn from you."

"I don't kiss and tell, angel. And *someone* has been rather unashamedly protecting my virtue by scaring off anyone she doesn't like. I've dated *two* people in my life. They were the only ones that got by you."

Her lower lip stuck out a bit in a pout. "I have better taste than you do." She refrained from mentioning her bitter jealousy that those two had gotten past her at all. "Kiss me." She tilted her face up invitingly, as naturally as a night-blooming rose sought the moon.

He cupped her cheek and leaned down to tenderly take her lips with his. She tasted of roses and incense. Felt as soft as rose petals. Need coiled hard inside his body, and he forced himself to keep the kiss light and gentle. He saw her iridescent eyes darken with the same desire he felt, and she leaned up into the kiss. Her lips parted under his.

A naturally sensual angel. He was a doomed man. He tugged her closer and deepened the kiss as she had asked. His tongue teasingly sought hers, and she returned the little caress without hesitation. Her hands settled over his heart as if staking a claim. They slowly eased apart and stared at each other. "Better?" he asked her huskily.

She stared at him with frustratingly sexy eyes and then surged up and kissed him hungrily. He dragged her closer and the embrace lost all semblance of control. The kiss deepened and deepened until he unexpectedly tasted a crackle of fire and lightning and knew he had found her soul. She took a little breath of surprise, and he almost lifted his head. Her arms swiftly banded around his neck to keep him close, and her mouth went wild under his. His arms shot around her waist and he hauled her off her feet. Her body pressed against his, and it felt nearly perfect against him. *Two years*, a little voice whispered in his mind. *Two years, she will be an adult.*

It was when she felt her wings stirring inside her soul that she realized she was in real trouble. She wanted to give him her wings. The urge alone told her that he would be her destined mate, but she was only sixteen! Either she was an early bloomer, or she was more deviant than they had always known.

He felt the sudden fear inside her and quickly lifted his head. His entire body ached painfully, and seeing the flush to her face and the way her eyes had darkened with shadowy power did nothing to help his control. Her breaths came as quickly as his did. "Good first kiss?" he asked her thickly.

She pressed trembling fingers to hers lips. So much for knocking off her socks. He had blown them to bits instead. "You win for best first and second kiss. I, uhm, am going to go. Take a shower. Cold one." She carefully backed away. It was tempting. It was really, really tempting to ask him to be her first lover. He would do it. And he would absolutely make it worth it. She just didn't trust herself to control her wings. Two years. She would know in two years.

She hastily whirled and rushed out of the library, and she didn't even see her father as she ran past him. Malthus eyed her back and then walked into the library. He took one look at Alexander and winced with wry humor and sympathy. "I believe I've said this before, but, you're a mess, kid."

Alexander didn't look up from where he had sat down. "No shit. It's still your daughter's fault. Please take this as it's meant: your daughter is absolutely lethal."

Malthus did his best not to laugh. "Alexander, I just want to tell you that Alyenna and I accept anything and everything that may or may not come to pass between you and Mai either now or in the future. Clear?"

He straightened and raked a hand through his tangled brown hair. "Clear. You can hold your blessings until she hits final maturity, however. I think she and I are both wary of her Flare. She's not . . . normal, still, for an angel." He glanced up. "I was able to kiss her soul."

Malthus blinked. "Well." It was unheard of for an angel's soul to be developed enough before maturity for his or her mate to find it via a mere kiss. He finally smiled ruefully. "That's Maitena for you. Always keeping us on our toes." He coughed. "You may want a cold shower."

"Will it work?"

"No, not really."

"Figures."

3
Shadow under the Sun

Mai and Eliana's Flares ended when they turned seventeen and began the short year toward maturity. Eliana went down to a relatively normal royal angel's level of appeal. Mai did not. While she did stop Flaring, she still had twice the impact of Eliana or even Josh. People would feel instant desire for her on first meeting unless she managed to crank down the volume. Perhaps as an apology for her appeal being so over the top, she actually *had* the ability to turn it up or down to some degree. She could keep it to a dull roar so people only just stopped and stared.

Josh hit final maturity at eighteen and settled into his power with grace. His green eyes turned to iridescent gold like his father's had at the same age, marking him as the heir to the Crystal Kingdom, but that was the only outward change. Things were surprisingly low-key overall for him hitting maturity. Then again, Laila was only fifteen. Josh had plenty of patience to spare and was willing to wait to be sure if she was his destined mate. Three years was not too long to endure if it meant waiting for his ultimate happiness.

The poor twins hit their Flare the year after he hit maturity. It could have been quite simple for them if they would pick a target, yet the only target either wanted was the one they had convinced themselves they should not have. They locked down instead and refrained from going out in public together. It only helped a bit. Sami had to enlist Kayden's aid in keeping them healthy, but that did not actually do her any good. Kev adamantly refused to let Kayden guard him—and it was a very telling thing. Mai immediately bent Kev's ear and gave him a blistering lecture. If he had the hots for Kayden, he ought to just give in and enjoy it. She envied him that opportunity, really.

Amusing one and all, it turned out that she was not actually affected in the slightest by the twins' Flare. They immediately began spending most of their time with her, preferring her company over any guardian or family member . . .

especially Kayden and Josh. The high prince took it with humor. He knew damned well he was giving Laila issues, and that didn't bother him at all. She had given him plenty already.

A month after the twins' Flare started, Eliana hit final maturity. She also settled into her power comfortably, and she made good on her promise. The very morning of her birthday, she literally tripped her guardian to the floor and pinned him down until he looked her in the eye and accepted what she had known all along about their destiny. Alyenna and Malthus were not surprised either, and they happily began planning a royal wedding.

A month later than that, Mai should have hit final maturity.

Should have.

She did not. By that point, after all the other strange things going on, no one really could be too surprised. Her eyes stubbornly remained green, rather than the silver they should turn as her mother's heir, and she did not cement into her power. She continued on just as she had the year before.

It left her and Alexander mutually miserable. Their desire for each other had not ended with Flare. It simply continued to steadily grow over time. They both fought to keep it hidden; what they already had between them was too precious to both of them to dare risk losing. It was the entire reason why they were holding out for her maturity at all.

She did not hit maturity at nineteen either. Alyenna's heart broke over her beloved daughter's misery, so she sent for Sami to come examine Mai. There had to be *something* going on! Sami was the strongest healer in either kingdom other than Mai herself; if Sami could not figure it out, then no one else ever could. She was their only hope.

When Sami arrived and walked into the drawing room where Mai waited, she saw the princess standing at the window. The sunlight made her glow brightly and beautifully, but it looked . . . a bit stifled somehow.

Sami walked over to her side and looked out the window. Alexander was with the twins in the gardens below. Kev had been dogging his heels to learn advanced magic. Laila wanted to learn more about swords. Their Flare had ended the month prior, and they were steadily approaching maturity, so they wanted to study more. Alexander had taken them under his wing, so to speak.

"I love him, Sami," Mai murmured.

Sami looked at her. "I had noticed. Trust me."

She closed her eyes. "The most important

person in my life. It would be so much simpler if I did not want him the way I do."

"Life would be much simpler without desire at all, but perhaps far more unenjoyable." Sami tugged her over to a chair and made her sit down. "Maitena," she sighed it, "speaking as his best friend and a royal guardian, he is your destined mate. Whether your final maturity tells you or not, you may as well give in now, and both of you be much happier."

"Sami." Mai didn't look up. "Did you know that sometimes an unrequited love appears between guardian and angel?"

"Yes, of course."

"Did you know that it can literally evaporate when the angel hits maturity?"

She said nothing for long moments, then, "No, actually, I did not. I see." That certainly explained why Alexander and Mai were trying to be so careful. On the other hand, Sami was *positive* that they were mates. It had been there long before Mai had ever hit puberty let alone started Flaring. It had merely grown along with her. Still, Sami could not blame them. Their relationship was already profound. "May I say only one more thing? I promise it will be my last word on it."

"Of course."

"I still think you need to give in and seduce

Alex if only to make him less inclined to take out his frustration on me, Kayden, and Maduin."

She started laughing. "You did not just tell me that. If you're that worried, take him into the city to the brothel." Under her breath, she muttered, "But don't tell me if you do. I'd probably kill an undeserving mortal."

"I offered three years ago," Sami admitted bluntly. Mai stared at her, and she smiled wryly. "While you were in Flare. He refused." She cuffed Mai's chin. "He's waiting for you, Mai. Now let's see if we can figure out how long this wait will be. Turn around."

Mai swung around and Sami lightly pressed her hands to her back. The skin was taut in a familiar way that meant Mai's wings were moving beneath, and Sami could certainly feel the snap of her power pressing against its current limitations. All of that was perfectly normal for an angel on the cusp of maturity. What was *not* normal was the lockdown she got an impression of inside Mai. "Huh." She sat back.

Mai turned around. "What is it?"

"There's some strange . . . lock inside you. For whatever reason, nature itself has stopped you from reaching final maturity at eighteen." She frowned thoughtfully. "I'm beginning to think it might be deliberate. You know how an angel who goes without Awakening for too long will release massive quantities of power?"

Mai's eyes widened. "For whatever reason, I'm being forced to reach a point where maturity will cause me to release some shockwave. But *why*, Sami? Why has any of this been happening to me? Why can't I be normal?"

"I don't know." She sighed and hugged Mai when the angel threw her arms around her. "I am sorry, Maitena. All I can assume is that it has to do with the Shadow element inside you. Whenever you finally, blessedly, reach maturity, we will have our answers." She smiled and eased Mai back. "Now, on a lighter note, did I hear correctly that Aya will be moving into the castle as an official member of the family?"

Mai grinned. "You did! She's always been more like a little sister to me than merely a second cousin, and she's a Shaman too." She fluttered her lashes. "She'll arrive next year, just a month before the twins hit final maturity. She had her own recently. She avoided Flare, the lucky thing, but she definitely still hit final maturity, so she will most assuredly know her destined mate on sight. You had better make arrangements with Kayden."

Sami smiled. That was more like their Mai. She was always the first to meddle and play matchmaker. She should have been the Goddess of Love. It was just a damned shame that her own love affairs could not be so easily sorted.

Aya did indeed come out the following year, and she took up residence in the Crystal palace as a member of the royal family. Mai and Alexander didn't bother to waste time or words. The same week Aya arrived, Mai grabbed her and literally dragged her into the grand hall just as Alexander literally dragged Sami in from the outside. Aya and Sami's eyes met, and the answer was there as had always been known. It was that look into the eyes—all the way into a soul—that could trigger the recognition of destined mates.

The arrangements had already been in place and pending. Sami's guardian duties were turned over to Kayden so she could guard Aya instead, who had actually never had a guardian because of her thin blood. The twins were ecstatic over the change if only because they loved Sami like she was their sister, and they wanted her happy. The only itsy-bitsy problem for the twins was that Kev still had the hots for Kayden, and having Kayden as a guardian meant Laila couldn't avoid Josh as much as she wanted. All of their parents sat back and prepared to enjoy the fireworks.

The fireworks started the day the twins turned eighteen. Josh had waited long enough. He went hunting for Laila the very morning of the event. The younger angel wasn't stupid. She made a beeline for the tree house in the gardens where she could safely hide. She yanked up the ladder behind her as a warning.

Josh just sighed as he stood at the bottom of the tree. "Laila. Seriously. Is it *really* that distasteful at the idea I might be your destined mate? Do you hate me?"

"No," came the mutter.

"Think I'm ugly?"

"Of course not!"

"In any way have objections to the fact that I am older, more powerful, and capable of kicking your ass as a Warrior?"

"Well, kind of, but, *no.*"

He lifted a brow. "Then what the *hell* is your problem, damn it? If you try to tell me you're not as absolutely miserable as I am, I'm going to break a family rule and call my cousin a liar!"

The near wail came from the treetop, "I don't want to be a queen!"

He dropped his head into his hands. "Oh, for crying out loud. Is *that* all? Shit, Laila. You know that I'm the one who will be doing all the work."

"Bullshit! Aunt Gillian is always working just as hard as Uncle Anthony!" Though, technically, Gillian and Anthony were technically cousins once removed to the twins, the age gap made it easier to just call them aunt and uncle.

"Okay, point conceded." He opened his wings, and he was entirely bemused that Laila had forgotten angels could fly. "But the burdens will still be mostly on me." He flew up, peeked in the window, and saw Laila looking warily out the other window. Silently, stealthily, he crept into the tree house.

Laila didn't know he was there as she warily kept watch out the window. She loved Josh more than *anything*, even her own twin. She just knew for a fact that he was hell on wheels, would always get his way, and trying to help him run the kingdom would absolutely be a nightmare!

She had always been very happy to be a lesser royal; she really didn't want to be a queen. She had ached watching Josh grow up under the expectation of ruling. He said he was perfectly fine with it, but she knew he was always happier when he could get away. She was stupidly in love with her cousin, and she knew it. Stupid destiny.

The touch of an Air element reached her just before arms shot around her waist. "Gah!" The tussle lasted less than a second, and she found herself flat on the ground with Josh pinning her down. "Damn it, Joshua!" she snarled. "You can be such a jerk!" She kept her head stubbornly turned. She would *not* look into those sexy gold eyes and be doomed.

"Laila." It was said achingly. "I need you at my side. Please. I've been waiting so long for this."

Her heart broke. She slowly turned her head and looked up into his eyes. The detonation was hard and fast, sweeping from her soul outward until her wings and body ached with violent, greedy desire. Red color moved through her eyes even as green moved through his, evidence of their Fire and Air elements responding as well. She could not fight her wings' demand, and they opened out into a spread position under her where they shimmered in the soft light.

Josh lowered his head until their lips were a breath apart. "You are my destined mate. Nothing else matters but this, Laila."

"You're such a pain," she groused against his lips. "I'm going to spend all my time trying to keep you from doing something stupid."

He grinned. "Yeah." He lowered his forehead to touch hers. "You're not stressing over my betrothal to Mai, are you?"

"Eh, I was never really jealous. For one thing, it was always conditional on you and her being or not being mates." She winced wryly. "For another, would you believe she actually pulled me aside a few years ago to tell me in no uncertain terms that she would not marry you because it would be 'immoral in her brain'?"

He had to laugh. "I believe it. I said something similar to her while she was in Flare." He skimmed his lips over Laila's and savored the way her breath caught. He had waited his entire life for that moment.

"B-but, what about the alliance?" She was fast losing the ability to think at all.

"Covered." He nibbled at her jaw. "Maduin has Summerwing blood, and Eliana has Everbird blood. When they get married next month, the alliance will be considered concrete. Destiny provides, Laila."

She muttered a single explicitly rude word and then turned her head and found his lips with hers. Stupidly in love. No better phrase existed for the way destined mates could never live without each other. "Don't you dare seduce me up here!" she groused when the kiss finally broke. "We won't live it down."

"Nobody will know." His fingers were already nimbly unbuttoning her shirt.

"Yes they will!" She groaned when hot hands moved over her skin. "You won't always get your way!"

"I'm a future king. Sure I will."

On the other side of the palace grounds, Kev was in both a better position and yet also worse position than his sister. He had managed to evade Kayden all morning, but his guardian always knew where to find him. It really wasn't fair of destiny to make a guardian be an angel's destined mate. And, yes, he suspected that that was what Kayden was to him.

It just didn't seem right! Kayden had been an adult before Kev had even hit Awakening, and he was powerful, strong, and incredibly gentle. The gentle giant, Kev often thought of him. He stood at a surprisingly tall six-six height and was overall large with it. He was also the gentlest and sweetest person Kev had ever known. At least until the twins or Josh got themselves into trouble. Kayden put up with a lot of their antics, but letting them get into danger was a big button for the guardian.

He was also ridiculously gorgeous. Kev peeked cautiously down the hall he was in and then sighed and leaned against the wall. It would be more fair to make bigger people less beautiful because they had more landscape, but in Kayden's case, nature had gleefully put every inch to good use. Kev loved his pale hair and auburn eyes, and he would have to have been absolutely blind to miss his sculpted guardian body.

The one he loved most. He was never happier than near Kayden. But a fourteen year age gap! Kayden couldn't possibly be his destined mate. It had to be unrequited.

"Kev."

He gulped and opened his eyes to see familiar boots. He slowly lifted his gaze and found himself looking at his very patient guardian. His green eyes skittered away before they met Kayden's auburn ones. "I didn't do it. Whatever happened was Laila's fault."

Kayden just smiled. "You can't blame her this time, Kev." He pressed a hand against the wall and leaned in. "You're breaking my heart, Kev," he said softly. "It kills me to watch you run from me. Why are you so afraid? You went to Sami for your first kiss and not me." His hand curled into a fist. "I almost broke her nose."

"I just . . ." How the hell was he supposed to say that he just didn't feel he deserved Kayden? A man who had worked his way up from being a servant to being a royal guardian that everyone admired and respected? Kayden was his *idol.*

His eyes moved out the window, and he spotted Mai arriving with Alexander, Sami, and Aya. They were there for the birthday party for the twins. The others would be arriving within another hour or so.

"Kev."

"I'm in love with Mai!" he blurted.

Kayden straightened and backed up quickly. He knew it was certainly plausible. Angels could love someone that wasn't their destined mate; they just wouldn't love that person with their *soul*. They would never be truly, deeply, eternally happy. And, certainly, Mai had always been a favored person of both twins.

His hands slowly curled into fists at his side as possessive fury churned. He had very nearly walked away before he realized Kev would *still* not look him in the eye. If he was in love with Mai and didn't think Kayden was his destined mate, why would he fear meeting his gaze? His angel was downright terrified, and, realizing it, Kayden's anger melted. Final maturity, and what came between destined mates, could be just as terrifying as what happened during a Flare. Maybe more.

Kev gulped as Kayden turned and walked away. He needed to get to Mai first and ask her to go along with things to give him some breathing room!

Kayden knew more shortcuts than he did, and he had longer legs to boot. He strode into the grand hall where the arrivals were taking off their coats and told Mai without preamble, "Kev says he's in love with you."

Mai's jaw dropped, and Aya about fell over. Alexander's initial surprise was shortly overwhelmed by fury, and his eyes darkened warningly. Sami hastily grabbed his arm. "Let's get a drink. Kayden, come with us." She dragged her best friend quickly down the hall, and Kayden followed along.

Mai and Aya were left behind, and they could only stare at each other. What the *hell* was going on in this castle?

Sami stopped dragging Alexander once they were in another room. Alexander barely spared her a look as he narrowed his eyes at Kayden. "Tell me why I should not find Kev and clip his wings." Magic moved across his eyes. "Maitena belongs to *me*, whether she is in final maturity or not. I won't allow a rival any more than she would."

"Easy." Kayden held up his hands. "There's no rivalry. Kev was lying. Well, technically, not lying. He does love her a great deal." He sighed and raked a hand through his hair. "I am Kev's destined mate, and he won't seem to tell me why he's afraid of such a thing." He scowled at Sami. "He went to you for his first kiss."

"And it was relatively awkward on my side as well," she retorted. "I *tried* to tell him to go to you, especially because he was already attracted to you, but he's as stubborn as any angel. Gets his willpower from his father, for certain." She pinched the bridge of her nose. "Of course he would just have to make things more complicated than they are. Tell me, at the least, Laila and Josh are fine."

"Trust me when I say to not go near the tree house in the East Garden."

Alexander snorted softly as his anger went away entirely. In its place came sympathy for Kev. It was, indeed, a scary time. "Josh cornered her?"

"He had to. The twins are too much alike." Kayden eyed him. "Would Mai go along with Kev's farce to help him?"

He snorted again. "She'd sooner tear a strip off his hide for being an idiot and probably tell him to come jump you and just get over it."

Mai and Aya had parted ways in the hall so that the younger cousin could find the party room where she could add their gifts to the pile. Mai instead headed for the pond in the West Gardens for some much needed fresh air. She chose the West Gardens deliberately since she had sensed a certain *merging* of power as soon as she was on the castle's grounds. She wasn't an idiot.

As she was skipping a stone across the pond, she sensed Kev approach. She turned and eyed him. "You are not in love with me."

He sighed as he stopped beside her. "No."

"Annnd . . . ?"

He scowled. "Can't you just go along with things? Pretend to be interested back and give me some room to breathe?"

"Would you like to tell me *why*?"

"I think Kayden is my destined mate." He raked a hand through his unruly brown hair in agitation. "He's too much older than me. He's too good for me, Maitena! He's worked for his station. What the hell have I ever done?"

She contemplated shaking him. "You should be *happy* that someone as incredible as Kayden is your destined mate. You get to have a guardian and a lover all rolled up in one. Just go jump him and get it over with! I am absolutely not getting in the middle! We've all known all along he was going to be your mate!"

He shot a glare at her. "You're one to talk, you know! We've all known Alexander was *your* mate! If you'd just hurry up and hit maturity, then you'd figure it out too!"

"You think I'm doing this on purpose?" she shouted at him. She gave him a little shove. "It's killing me! I don't know who or what I am! Nothing I ever do is normal! I love him so much and I can't be with him! You're the idiot who won't take what destiny has given!"

His own temper flared in return. "Maybe you should stop worrying about destiny and stop being stupid yourself! You'd make everyone a lot happier if you'd just jump your damn guardian and be done with it!"

"You don't know *anything*!" Her temper spiked, and with it came her magic. Shadowy power welled up around her body and slapped Kev so hard that it threw him into the pond. He surfaced and stared at her in shock, and her stomach churned. "Oh god. Oh god. Kev, I'm sorry. I didn't intend . . . didn't mean . . ." She stared at her hands. She had no control. She whirled and ran away as fast as she could.

Kev felt nothing but pain as he watched her flee. Not physically. She hadn't actually done any damage to him. He hurt *for* her. It was just too damned cruel of destiny and nature, what they were doing to her. He also felt like a complete jerk for lashing out at her the way he had. She hadn't deserved that. He owed her a big apology.

"Stepped in it, didn't you?"

He sighed as he saw Kayden standing on the side of the pond. "Yeah. Apparently being an adult doesn't curb the ability to be an ass to someone who doesn't deserve it." He gingerly made his way to the slippery edge of the pond but sighed again as he couldn't get a grip to pull himself out. "Damn it, I can't get out."

Kayden crouched down. "Good. That gives me a chance to talk to you without you running away. Would you like to tell me what you're so worried about, Kev? Why would you lie to me like that?"

"I don't deserve you."

It was said so softly that Kayden almost missed it. When it registered, he blinked in confusion. Surely he had heard wrong. "Pardon?"

A hint of red climbed Kev's neck. "You're fourteen years older than me. You've worked hard for where you are. You're my *hero*, Kayden. I haven't done anything at all. I just don't deserve you."

Kayden's sigh was long. "Alexander is twelve years older than Mai, and I believe I just heard you yelling at our favorite princess that she should really give in and jump him."

Kev sank down deeper in the water. His cheeks felt red-hot. "Okay, now I really feel like an idiot. And a hypocrite. Also, I'm freezing."

Kayden bit back a smile as he reached down and lifted his shivering angel out of the pond. "Let's get you inside and warmed up." He started to walk away when a hand grabbed the back of his tunic. "Yes?"

"Kayden?"

He slowly turned around. "Ask and it's yours, Kev. You know that." Hesitant green eyes slowly lifted to meet his, and the detonation tore through them equally. The fiercest urge to bind Kev's wings to him so he could not fly away filled

Kayden. The desire he had long accepted turned into an inferno there could be no ignoring. He saw red power moving through Kev's darkened eyes and felt magic sting the air. He slowly reached out to frame Kev's face with one gentle hand. "I love you," he said softly, firmly. "I have all along. *I* don't deserve *you*, Kev Sheridan. No one ever deserves an angel."

Kev took a little breath and then surged up and kissed his guardian the way he had wanted for years. He was a little less than a foot shorter than Kayden, and he absolutely loved it. He loved how safe his guardian could make him feel. The sight of orange Sun power moving through Kayden's beautiful eyes made his entire body clench harder with need. The one he loved most. Wanted most. There was no one else. The sheer *joy* in his soul was both elating and terrifying. "I love you," he said thickly against Kayden's lips when they parted. "And I'm sorry I'm an idiot."

"I still love you." Kayden carried him along toward the palace. "And you still need to get cleaned up before the party. You're soaking wet and still shivering."

"I'm not convinced the shivering isn't because of you. Also, a lot of the kelp on me is now on you. You're kinda messy too, Kayden. Maybe you should, you know, shower with me."

Kayden's lips curved. "We might be late to

your party."

"It's my party. I'm entitled. And Laila will absolutely be late as well. We're angels. Final maturity. I think our parents would be *glad* for why we were late." He grinned. "I still stand by my earlier statement that Mai will be happier when she gives in to Alexander. Can I go back to yelling at her later? It won't be hypocritical anymore." His guardian just laughed, and he held on contentedly. His hero. Finally his.

Alexander calmly walked through the castle toward the secret rooms that the angels thought they were the only ones to know about. The guardians had always known; they had just always let their angels be alone if they chose to hide there. He would be damned if he let Mai hide from him this time. He had seen the scene from a window, and he would have felt her power anyway.

He found the door hiding behind a tapestry and pushed it open to duck inside. The room beyond was quite small at barely seven feet in length and width. It was not even really a room; it was one of the inevitable pockets of unused space in such a large structure. The Chalice Kingdom had them too. Curled up in a corner, her face buried in her knees, was his angel. She was trying to cry silently, and her entire body shook.

"Butterfly." He walked over and sat down beside her.

"Don't touch me!" she whispered. She hiccupped on the last word. "I could've killed Kev! I don't want to hurt you too!"

"You can't hurt me." He lifted her onto his lap and enfolded her within his arms and cloak. Though she had not formally hit final maturity, she was still fully-grown now. Her body fit into his arms as if she had always belonged. "Here," he murmured. "Better?"

She curled as close as she could to him. She would have crawled into his soul if she could, just to let his beautiful light and dark surrounded her. She knew he was both. She knew his magic covered all elements the way hers did. He was not Shadow, but he was something different. Something truly beautiful to her. The light inside him was what let her see hope, and the dark inside him was what let her rest. She loved him so terribly. If she lost that at final maturity, she would die anyway.

The tears continued to well without stop. She turned her face into his shoulder and let them come. If he held her, she couldn't break. There had to be a reason to her power. She just didn't know what it was. What if she never found control? She might destroy the one thing in her life worth living for: her guardian. She did not have memories without him. He had held her hand for her first steps, and it had been into his arms she had first flown. His name had been her first word. Her everything. He was the biggest part of her existence. She could not risk losing him.

Things seemed to settle down to some extent. Word of the incident had spread across the world, and people began to murmur again about the Shadow Elemine. The speculation this time was far more focused as people wondered if, perhaps, the princess herself *was* the Shadow Elemine. Only final maturity might bring that answer, and the people prayed for that moment to come for *her* sake. There was no one who did not know how miserable she and her guardian were as they waited for destiny to confirm what everyone knew.

Mai's twentieth birthday came up, and a banquet was held as normal. It was a relatively small affair for her sake; she had been much more cautious around people lately. Only the two kingdoms and a few select nobles were invited. She did manage to enjoy herself quite a bit, and she proved she was still their Mai by telling Laila, "You have a hickey."

Laila hastily clapped a hand over her neck as

she heard everyone, including her parents, laughing. "Damn it, Maitena!" She scowled at her friend. "Why do you always tease me?"

Mai kissed her cheek. "Because of many weird and complicated ways that you are unfortunately related to me and therefore like my little sister." She swung an arm around Laila's waist companionably. "Kev gave Kayden one, too. I intend to embarrass him at the dinner table. You'll be even."

Laila just snorted. There was no way to *not* love Mai. She kept an arm around Mai's waist in turn as they headed toward the buffet. A strange shade began to creep through the area, and she looked up quickly. "Whoa."

Mai followed her gaze and so did everyone else. Silence fell as everyone realized there was an eclipse occurring. There had not been one of any shape or form for almost exactly twenty years. It was a moment of perfect suspension when light and dark met and melded.

Alyenna looked at her daughter and suddenly paled. "Alexander," she whispered. "Alexander, hurry!"

He was already running across the ground. "Laila! Get away from Mai!"

Shadowy power erupted around Mai as the eclipse settled fully and the Earth entirely blocked the sun. The onslaught of her power broke free with such force that Laila was sent head over heels across the ground. Josh and Kayden managed to catch her, and she shrugged them off. "I'm fine!" The burns across her arm and the scrapes from the fall implied otherwise, but she vehemently shook her head. "What's wrong with Mai?"

The power blazed hotter and hotter and brighter and brighter until a shockwave ripped from Mai's body as she gave a pained cry and Firai crackled into the air around her. Everyone recognized that cry. The sound of angel entering final maturity or Awakening after far, far too long.

"Alex!" Sami grabbed her friend's arm before he could rush in. "She might kill you! She's all elements! She's Shadow!"

"I don't care!" he snarled. He ripped his arm free and plunged past the blazing light to where Mai stood. She collapsed into his arms and clung onto his cloak with desperate strength. She stared up at him for a long moment before her eyes suddenly turned silver. In that moment, even in the shade, her halo *burned* in a way it never had before.

"Final maturity," Robert managed to whisper. "She reached final maturity." He hastily grabbed Malthus' arm before he could run forward. "Sami's right, Mal! She could kill someone with that much raw elemental power!"

Mai went limp in Alexander's grip, and he knelt down to gently place her on the grass. He wrapped his cloak around her tightly and continued to hold onto her through the waves of elemental power. He weathered the storm calmly and without harm. He did not care if everyone knew he had multi-elemental magic of his own. Nothing was in his world but his angel. She needed him.

When Fire rose, he put it out with the tides of Water. When Air's wind blew too hard, he grounded it with land-based Sand. When the Sun blazed too brightly, he darkened it with the Moon. It then went back the other way. Whatever tore out of her, he was able to tame. Her Shadow power rose at the end, hotly and alarmingly, but he felt a stirring of unusual and new magic inside that would perfectly match. He reached for it without hesitation, and a surge of silvery power swept around him. It met the Shadow and gently enfolded it so that it tamed and calmed without any trouble.

The storm passed as swiftly as it had happened. Though the eclipse remained, the power did not. Mai slipped into a peaceful sleep in Alexander's arms as everyone watched without words. She looked impossibly more beautiful than the others had ever seen her before. She truly transcended beauty itself.

Into the eerie silence, Aya said softly, "Evil comes."

Sami turned quickly and discovered that her angel's eyes had dilated until there was no telling her pupils from her iridescent blue eyes. "Aya." She gently took her shoulders and reached for her through their souls. It would ground Aya and give her the strength to see what her Sight demanded. "What do you see?"

"Evil comes for the one of Shadow." She barely saw her lover. Her eyes were fixed on her cousin. "It knows she lives. The Shadow Elemine. She must awaken. Our world will be destroyed if she does not." She blinked and her eyes went back to normal. "Ooh. My head." She dropped her aching head onto Sami's shoulder. "Mai." Her lips trembled. Why did it have to be Mai?

A soft swirl of light had everyone looking up, and the light formed into the heraldic shield representing the Elemine. "Send her to us," a male voice said. "I am the Moon Elemine. I speak for my brothers and sisters. Send her to us. We can awaken her. Our world will be doomed if she does not." As the light faded, his voice added softer, "I'm sorry."

Alyenna's hands clenched together as she walked forward. "Alexander, take Maitena to her tower. Do not leave her side until she awakes. Bring her to us when she does. Anthony, come with me. We must discuss what this means for our kingdoms." She swept a warning look over the entire area. "Nothing that happened here will leave this garden. All anyone knows is that the princess hit final maturity. Anthony and I will determine what is best for our lands and my child. The rest of you are to go home." She turned toward the castle with her chin held high. Evil would not take her people, and it especially would not take her daughter.

Anthony joined her, and she glanced back to see Alexander carrying Mai away. Silver magic. Of course. It made sense of many things she had always wondered. "Infinity," she murmured.

"Indeed," he said just as softly. "There is a reason for every birth, Aly. I suppose we are now learning what Mai's is." He followed her gaze and added quieter, "And Alexander's as well. But there is a bright side to all this."

"Yes?"

"She hit final maturity. They'll be much easier to live with."

She had to smile. He was as incorrigible as his son.

4
Shadowy Lover

Mai slowly drifted up out of a dreamless sleep and felt her soul throbbing in a way that meant it was still healing from her maturity. She also felt slightly foggy and disoriented, but she clearly remembered most of what had happened. She would rather have not. She could have killed Laila, and she felt a little sick remembering how Alexander had held her together. He could have been killed, too.

The familiar scent of apples drifted to her as the fragrance of one man's skin. Alexander. She knew he was there even before the bed shifted and he sat beside her. She opened her eyes and found herself staring up into his darkened violet eyes. Her breath hitched as that incredible, long-awaited, firestorm of greedy desire ripped through her body and soul until her wings throbbed and her magic churned inside her blood. She saw his eyes darken more and silvery power move in their depths as it claimed him too, and her lips trembled as she tried to smile. "I love you," she whispered achingly. "I've waited too long for you. I feel like I've waited millennia for you."

He cupped her cheek as he leaned in closer. The torrent of need inside him was not new. It was wonderfully familiar. He wanted nothing more than to wrap himself within her arms, to fuse her wings into his soul where she could never fly away from him. "Butterfly." It was barely breathed against her lips. "I have loved no one else. My angel."

She surged up and kissed him with all the unleashed force and fury of her newly matured soul. The kiss deepened in a heartbeat until he again tasted the potent power inside her. He had craved that flavor for four years. His fingers buried into her thick hair as he fed from her mouth. She moaned softly and it was music on his ears.

They slowly parted to draw in air, and she did not care that all of her longing was in her eyes. "Alex." She frowned as he suddenly stood. "Where are you going?"

"To take a relatively useless cold shower."
He didn't turn. "I was to bring you downstairs
when you woke, angel. There are things we have
to talk about." He took a step toward the door
and then stopped abruptly as magic smashed into
the lock and melted it. He whirled quickly and
found her standing beside her bed, gray magic
moving over fingers. "Maitena."

"I have waited years for you!" she said
fiercely. "My parents can damned well wait their
turn!" She leapt up into his arms and caught his
face in her hands as she kissed him wildly. She
poured herself into it so hotly that her gray wings
flew open and arched magnificently. They glowed
as bright as the halo around her body.

It would take a far, far stronger man than
him to turn down a beautiful angel when she
offered herself so freely. He dragged her even
closer and took control of the kiss from her. He
was only happy when he could taste the fire and
lightning inside her. He felt her hands yanking at
his tunic and very nearly laughed. "You want me
naked?" He hotly nipped at her slender neck.
"Should I give you a hickey to make Laila feel
avenged?"

She gave a sultry laugh that was easily the
most erotic thing he had ever heard. "I intend to
give you a few myself, to make sure others keep
their eyes off of my mate!" She leaned back

enough to nearly tear open the laces at the collar of his tunic. "I've wanted you naked for years." She groaned as she found a snug tank top under the tunic. "Why must you wear so many clothes?"

He dropped her onto the side of the bed and yanked off the tunic and then the tank top. The way she sighed made him feel infinitely desired and powerful. He leaned down to trap her against the covers, and her wings curled up to wrap around him in a mated angel's most possessive gesture. "Someone else wears far too much."

She nipped at his lip. "No one lets me run around naked. Said I'd blind people."

"I'm willing to risk it." He tugged at the laces of her bodice until he could peel it away. He unlaced her dress and pulled it down as well, and it was his turn to groan as he found a slip and a bra beneath. "Temptress. Packing all that beauty where I can't get to it easily."

"Seductress." She slowly ran her hands over his chest and nearly purred. He was hard and hot and wonderful. It had been self-inflicted torture to sneak off where she could watch him working out with the other guardians. He and Kayden often went shirtless when they went hand-to-hand against one another.

"What's the difference?" He lifted her to her feet and the dress fell to her ankles. His breath hissed in. The slip didn't go very far down her legs. She may have been little, but she was *perfection.*

"A temptress does naturally what a seductress does deliberately."

"The problem with you, my butterfly, is that you're both!"

She gave another breathless laugh when her slip literally came apart in his hands as he tugged too hard. "I can see myself explaining that one!" Nothing had ever felt more wonderful, more natural, than the desire that poured through her body. It shouldn't be possible that anything feel that good. His scent, his taste. The way his hands and hair felt. It was dizzying, drugging pleasure.

Hands yanked and tugged at remaining clothes until there was nothing left between them. She felt nothing but a surge of fierce need when she looked at him. He was beautifully, powerfully, aroused by her. Little scars flecked his nearly perfect beauty as reminder of the way he had willingly risked his life to keep her safe. His arms closed around her and tears burned her eyes. How could it be possible to love anyone as much as she loved him? For the first time, she better understood her own angelic life. If he left her, she would need no guardian to save her. There would be nothing left to save.

He lifted her up and dropped her on the

bed. "On you go." He pounced and made her laugh as he pinned her. "Better get on here before I take you on the floor."

"Can you try that later, maybe? The rug is pretty comfy."

His laugh was almost a groan as he kissed her again with an edge of desperation. "Later." His mouth rushed over her face. "Anytime. Maybe tonight. I think I'm addicted to you, Maitena."

She doubted there was anything sexier than her guardian out of control. She waited until he had kissed her again before letting her magic flood her mouth and froth into his. His entire body jerked against her, and his eyes glazed slightly. He broke free from the kiss to bury his lips between her breasts. "Dirty pool, angel!" He found a tight nipple begging for attention and closed his mouth hotly over it. She cried out softly, and he tugged just to savor her whimper. He lavished the same attention on her other breast, and his hands gently squeezed and caressed. She bit back another cry, and he teased huskily, "The tower is soundproof."

"Shaman!" It was gasped as one hand slid between her legs to stroke and torment her sensitive flesh. "Don't you dare make me scream! Eliana will never let me live it down!"

"Don't challenge your lover, angel." He

dragged her up to a sitting position and spun her around in his arms. "You gave her crap after she and Maduin became lovers. She's due some revenge." His mouth slid slowly down her back. "I've wanted to do this for years."

She cried out as his mouth found the pinfeathers on her back. There was no place more sensitive on an angel's body than the wings. Her fingers found his thighs and her nails dug in for balance as he zeroed in on every sensitive place of her wings. The pleasure went from wing to soul to womb to heart to every nerve until she was sobbing with each breath. "Stop!" Her head fell back helplessly as his mouth found the tender tendons where her wings folded. "Please!"

He cursed roughly as he turned her again and kissed her as deeply as he could. She wrapped her arms and legs around him desperately, and when that wasn't enough, her wings coiled around him as well. The feathers meshed and locked together in a way that could not be broken without tearing the wings from her back. The gesture was the last straw. He pressed her back to the bed and buried his aching flesh to the hilt inside her welcoming heat.

She arched eagerly beneath him to take him deeper, and he shuddered. Heaven. She felt like heaven. Destiny itself had put them together. A millennia of waiting. They had been lovers since the beginning of time. He drove into her again and again, greedily drinking her breathless whimpers from her mouth. "Give me everything!" he managed to say. He caught her face in his hands and made her look at him. "Give me everything!"

She couldn't have stopped herself. She reached for him with all of her power and her soul, poured herself into him until she could finally crawl into his soul and wrap him around her. She fused herself so thoroughly to him that he felt as if he could fly on her wings. He reached for her just as deeply and let his magic and soul and guardian power take her as deeply as he taken her body. Deeper until the glorious shadowy depths of her soul consumed him.

In that moment of fusion, ecstasy impacted and tore through them both in endless waves of wild pleasure. She probably would have screamed with it if he hadn't been kissing her again. The sound reverberated through his body with the potency of her magic, and they fell into that wonderful, glorious place only destined lovers could ever find.

He sank deeper into her arms and had just enough presence of mind to catch his weight on his arms before he cut off her air. Letting go was quite literally impossible with the way she was still wrapped around him. Her wings alone ensured he could not get free. Not that he really had any desire to do so.

She suddenly asked huskily into his shoulder, "Worth not going to that brothel?"

He had to laugh. "Damn Sami and her big mouth!" Her wings unlocked, and he slid his arms around her so that he could roll over onto his back. She sprawled contentedly across his chest with her head over his heart. "I waited seven years for you, Maitena," he told her softly, sincerely. "Once you hit puberty and I realized I wanted you, I was content to wait. You inadvertently made it much harder when you were sixteen, but I waited."

"I made something harder, for sure."

He snorted. His sultry, sassy, and naturally sensual angel would keep him on his toes for the rest of their lives, and he was perfectly fine with that. "I think we can concede that we probably could have just given in when you were sixteen and been less miserable these last few years."

She hid her face against his shoulder. "I was just too scared it might be another trick of destiny. I'm already so different, Alex. Why wouldn't I be wrong about my mate, too?" She rubbed her cheek slowly against his skin. "I'm still scared. What if I hurt you with my power?"

"You can't."

She lifted her head quickly and frowned.

"True. You did somehow absorb my power. I knew all along you were multi-elemental like me, and that you had Light and Dark as well. I just didn't think you could do what you did. You don't have Shadow."

"It would seem I have something else." He cupped her face in his hands. "Look inside me, butterfly."

She reached out lightly for the magic inside him and saw the familiar presence of Fire, Air, Moon, Sand, Sun, and Water. They were no longer alone for something new had been added. Something that was softly silver in color and felt like a blend of all the others in the way her Shadow power was. It felt endless and . . . infinite. Her breath hitched. "Infinity. You're an Infinity element." As understanding came, her eyes slowly widened. "No. No, you're more. If I am the Shadow Elemine then you are . . ."

He drew her down for a tender kiss. "Millennia," he murmured huskily against her lips. "We both felt it. We've waited millennia to be together." He smoothed her hair back. "I remember nothing. I only really understood my true power a few hours ago when I needed to save you from yourself. I am still your guardian. Your destined mate. Whatever we may have been before will not change what we are now."

Tears slid slowly down her cheeks as she

looked into his beloved eyes and saw the welcoming silvery power. "Only you," she whispered. "It was always only you." She held on as he turned and tumbled her onto the bed again. Her breath caught as his hands moved slowly over her body and relit the desire barely under the surface. "Aren't my parents waiting?"

"They can wait a while more. I've waited years for you." He kissed her again. His Elemine lover. He had truly, literally, been born to love her.

They eventually did get dressed again and go to the drawing room where her parents and Anthony waited. She held tight to Alexander's hand as she walked inside, and she was also wearing his cloak around her shoulders. She had on her favorite dress and bodice again, but she couldn't stop shivering with nerves. "Uhm." It was only Alexander's hand on hers that kept her from running. "Laila?"

"Is just fine," Anthony told her gently. "She is worried sick about you. She had nothing wrong that Sami could not mend." He smiled. "You look wonderful, sweetheart. Final maturity suits you."

Malthus looked at Alexander. "I've waited a long time to tell you this: welcome to the family, son." He saw Mai's shoulders relax and lightly chided her, "Don't give us that look, young lady.

We told you years ago that we were perfectly fine with what destiny had decided for you." He smiled. "Truly, we knew from the day you were born that he was the one for you."

"He means *I* knew," Alyenna corrected. She smiled at Alexander. "From the moment I called you to me, I already knew."

Alexander gently wrapped his arms around Mai's shoulders. "She was not yet born."

"And yet, every time I saw you at court, I could feel her stirring. She sensed you, my dear. You two have always belonged together." She patted the settee. "Now let's sit down and discuss why." Mai sat down beside her, and Alexander sat on Mai's other side. Alyenna took her daughter's hands and met her eyes directly. "You are the Shadow Elemine, Maitena."

Mai drew a long breath. "I actually remember most of what happened to me, Mother. People have been whispering that that might be what I am, and when I woke a while ago, I had to accept it as truth. Alex is . . ."

"We know." Anthony's voice was calm. "We noticed that when he saved you." He smiled. "We can see it more clearly now. The brand of his power left on you is that of Infinity, not Moon as he always pretended to be." He sat back in his chair on a sigh. "If only it could be that simple, that two Elemine were reborn. But it's not. Aya had a vision."

Her shoulders tensed and Alexander pulled her closer. "And?" she asked softly.

"She foretold of an evil coming to our world that will come for you. That only you can stop." Alyenna drew a deep breath. "After, the herald of the Moon Elemine arrived. He requested that you travel to the Temple of the Elemine to awaken in order to save our world. We would love to believe it is not truly terrible, but, the eclipse has lingered. Should it stay for too much longer, our world will begin to die. I do not know what evil has come, but it has indeed arrived."

Mai's chin lifted. "Then I will go." She met her mother's eyes. "What desire do I have to inherit a kingdom that rules over a dead world? If I can best serve my people by becoming an Elemine, then that is what I will do."

Alyenna nodded slowly. "We would not have asked you. We had decided to do whatever we could should you not wish the journey. The Temple of the Elemine is a few days away from here. Perhaps there, the Elemine will tell you what is happening to our world." She leaned over and gently kissed Mai's forehead. "I love you," she said softly. "You will always be my most precious gift."

Mai hugged her mother tightly and then ran over and hugged Malthus just as fiercely. He buried his face in her hair for a moment. His baby girl was his most precious gift as well. "Be safe," he murmured.

She hugged Anthony as well and then straightened. "I will leave at once."

"*We* will leave," her guardian corrected. She frowned at him and he lifted a brow. "You genuinely think that I am going to let you go alone? Maitena, I wouldn't have let you go alone *before* we were mates let alone now that we are."

She scowled at him. "Being my mate does not mean you have the right to order me around!"

He stood and scooped her up under one arm. "No. And neither does my being your guardian. I do it anyway because no one else dares." He ignored her kicking feet and hauled her out of the drawing room.

"Hey, Mal, haven't *you* done that to Aly before?" Anthony asked idly.

"Shut it," Alyenna muttered. She huffed as her husband and best friend both laughed at her. It wasn't *her* fault that her royal blood produced strong-willed and independent females! In fact, she was looking forward to seeing what sort of grandchild she got. It had been a very, very long time since human blood had been mixed in. Considering Alexander really was only two wings shy of being an angel himself, it would be very interesting indeed.

Alexander put Mai down in the hall and grinned when she glared at him. He flicked a finger down her nose. "Stop giving me the evil eye, angel." He kissed her softly until she melted against him on a sigh of delight. Her lashes lifted, and he admired her iridescent silver eyes. "I will meet you at the stables," he murmured huskily. "Should I tell someone to start moving my things to your room?"

"No," she said against his lips. She stepped back and shot a sultry smile over her shoulder. "I'll move into yours. Your bed is bigger."

He grinned wickedly as he headed down the hall. His mate had a pragmatic side that was surprisingly sexy. Who knew?

They met up in the stables an hour later. They had both packed backpacks with additional clothes, supplies, and food. More the last than anything else; angels are a *lot* compared to humans. Mai could eat more than Alexander did and she was half his size. It was the only way her body sustained her power safely. Food was consumed for her soul long before it reached her stomach.

Tynan was also going along, and he kept pace beside their horses without any problem though the effects of the eclipse were already spreading across the land. Monsters were not the only danger now. Normal animals had been driven mad and become a danger of their own. People were staying indoors for their own safety. The world that had just that morning been merry and cheerful had turned into a giant ghost town.

The trip was relatively easy, all things considered. The first two days were nothing to speak of in the end. Alexander was the human equivalent of a Shaman, and Mai *was* a Shaman. She was also a Summoner capable of calling elemental beasts to her side, and the combination was potent. The fact that she had healing power also helped. Nothing stayed injured for long. Tynan was also quite capable in combat, and he stayed at Mai's side when Alexander could not.

It was the third day when they were only a few miles away from the temple that things took a turn for the worse. Tynan had gone ahead of them, and Mai suspected he would be waiting at the temple. She and Alexander had briefly paused their horses to look for a campsite when a terrifying scream rose on the air. It startled the horses so violently that Mai's threw her from its back. She landed with a thump on the ground, and Alexander quickly dismounted to run to her side. "Angel!"

"Ow. I'm okay. Just sore." She let him tug her up to her feet, and her heart froze in terror. "Alex."

He looked up sharply as he felt the danger surrounding them, and he also stopped breathing for a moment. A horde. At least twenty monsters had crept out of the trees to surround them. The horses went running away in fear, and a few chased after them. The air crawled with the low sound of growling and a sort of sinister laugh.

Alexander would have, in a heartbeat, laid down his life for Mai. The terrible trouble with that would be that it would now doom her to death anyway. "Butterfly," he said in a low voice, "I want you to swear to me that if something happens, you will endure to save our world before you let Sami or Maduin send you to my side."

"You won't die!" she vowed fiercely. "I won't let you!"

"Your word, angel."

She choked back tears. It hurt to even think about. "I vow it." She caught a breath as she saw movement. "Alex!"

He drew the silver dagger at his side and matching silver magic swirled around the blade to make it into a sword. Mai drew the sword she also carried, and she wielded it with one hand as she palmed magic in the other. She whirled on the balls of her feet like a dancer and beat back anything that got too close. Sometimes a claw got through and she took the damage for it. She healed anything that bled too fast and ignored the rest.

A second wave of the horde arrived, and a sickening scent rose on the air with the putrid stench of massacre and bloody genocide. She gagged violently and dropped her sword as the smell seemed to rebel against the very essence of what she was. She staggered and fell to her knees as she fought whatever it was that was trying to cut her soul. Her head jerked up at a sound and she saw claws as long as a sword lunging for her face.

Alexander threw himself physically over her, and the claws gouged deep into his back. It could not stop him. He sprang to his feet and released a violent wave of silver magic that drove the horde back several feet. He promptly fell to his knees again with only his sword to hold him up, and Mai saw the nightmarish wound through his cloak and tunic.

Fury welled and she let out a piercing scream of rage. It carried all of her magic, and the horde immediately ran away with pained and terrified yips. Alexander looked at her and managed a smile. "For once, you actually listened to me."

She leapt forward and caught him as he fell, and she landed in the dirt in her efforts to hold him. She yanked away his cloak and nearly ripped his tunic and tank to reach the wound. It bled far too hard and fast. It was easily a foot long and crossed nearly the entirety of his back. She could see muscle and tissue, and his pain churned inside her own body. His soul yanked at hers as if he would leave her behind. *She would not let him go!*

A sudden soft green light began to filter through the air as a woman's voice murmured, *Shadow, you are the High Healer. You possess the greatest healing power in all of existence. You can heal him. No one else but you can. If there is a breath left, you can bring them back. Give him your breath and bring him back.*

Mai reached for Alexander through their bonds and forced his lungs to take the breath from hers. She reached down deeper and deeper into her soul until Light and Dark met and fused into the gray shadow of her true power. Healing magic poured through her blood and foamed over her hands as she began to carefully stitch the wound closed. "No more scars on this body," she murmured huskily. She felt his instant refusal, and her fingers paused as she realized he *wanted* to keep the scar. When he seemed as if he would actually try to block her magic in his efforts to keep it, she sighed. "You're going against everything that is a healer in me!"

Still, she closed the wound and left the scar. It made her feel a little sick to watch the thick mark mar such a beautiful expanse of skin. He stirred and carefully sat up, and he saw the tears in her eyes. He framed her face with his hands and eased in to kiss her. "I'm here," he breathed. "No tears."

"Let me take it away!" she whispered fiercely.

"No." He rubbed his thumb over her lips. "It is a badge of honor, angel. I earned it fighting for you. It is the mark that I am your guardian and no other. It brands me as yours alone. I am *honored* to be your guardian, Maitena. That scar shows my love for you."

"Show it with a wedding band or a hickey!" she shouted at him. "Not a scar!" Her words halted as he yanked her close and kissed her hard. She grabbed at him desperately and all but crawled into his soul to find his silvery infinite power. Only then did the panic finally let her go. He eased back, and she whispered, "Stubborn guardian."

"I love you." He kissed her again. "No more tears."

They were both a filthy mess but there wasn't much they could do about it. He pulled on a new tank top but didn't bother with a tunic. Instead, he pulled the tunic on over Mai's head. It was far too big but she didn't care. She just snuggled into it with a tactile delight that made his heart ache. He did put his cloak back on, and they both ignored the long tear in the back. As he was fastening the front, he smiled to see her picking up her sword. "I'm surprised you even remembered what I had told you."

"To scream my lungs off if I was ever in danger that neither you nor I could blast or hack my way out of?" she asked dryly. "Let's call it instinct more than remembering your instructions. I was just too pissed off that my mate was dying."

They rested only very briefly before continuing to the temple they could see rising above the trees in the distance. When they finally reached it, they discovered it to be a crumbling ruin of stone and mortar that had endured time painfully without anyone to care for it. It hurt both Mai and Alexander equally. Sitting just outside the entrance was the familiar form of Tynan. He slowly walked toward them and then light engulfed him and he began to change shape.

The light faded to leave behind a handsome young man who looked no older than Mai. Shaggy gray hair framed his face, and he stood a few inches shorter than Alexander with an overall more slender frame. It made him no less powerful, and the celestial Elemine symbol of Shadow was visible on his face.

He was not unfamiliar to Alexander nor was

he a surprise. The guardian merely smiled. "Did you ask Mai to dance with her, or was it her idea, Tynan?"

He smiled wryly. "A bit of both. I had wondered if you knew, Alexander."

"I was strongly suspicious, shall we say? I always knew you were sentient, and when I saw you that night, you were just familiar somehow." He kept his arm around Mai's shoulders. "Would you like to confirm who I now suspect you are?"

Tynan slowly went down onto one knee before Mai. "As is right of my sentient will, I pledge my life for the defense of yours, my Shadow Elemine." He lowered his head. "All Elemine have a guardian beast. I am yours if you will have me."

She shook her head fondly. "Tynan, you've been mine, and I've been yours, since the day you saved me and my stubborn guardian." She knelt down and wrapped her arms around his neck. "I am happy you have always been with me. I don't care why you are. I love you as if you were my brother. I accept that you see yourself as my 'beast' and that I am your master, but you must accept that I see you as my companion and friend."

His eyes softened as he hugged her back. The power of Shadow was that of love. No one but Mai could have ever been the Shadow

Elemine. She loved more than any other creature, and it was impossible to not love her in return. She brought joy to all those around her. Sharing the last fifteen years of her life had been a gift.

Alexander helped them both stand, and Tynan led the way into the temple. It was a relatively convoluted maze to reach the middle, but Tynan's steps didn't waver. In the very center of the temple was a large room with six altars circling a central one. Sitting on the altars around the edges were the six Elemine of the world.

They were all unusually beautiful, and their coloring matched to whatever element they embodied. They looked roughly the same age as Alexander though that was deceptive when they had existed for millennia. The eldest was technically the Moon Elemine. The sisters were Sand, Air, and Water. The brothers were Fire, Sun, and Moon. The sisters had a relatively delicate build, and the brothers were bigger. Each and every one of the Elemine bore an eerie resemblance to Mai . . . and Alexander.

The Air Elemine gave a squeal of sheer delight and surged forward in a swirl of wind to happily hug Mai around the neck. "I've wanted to see you again for so long!" she rushed. "You're here! You're here!"

Mai recognized her voice as the one who had told her of her healing power, and she smiled. "I'm here." She hugged Air back and then let go. She promptly laughed as the Fire Elemine grabbed her instead and swung her around. All of the Elemine needed to hug her, and she couldn't help but feel as if she was reuniting with lost children. The feeling was compounded when all of the Elemine also hugged Alexander, much to his bemusement.

"Let's settle down," the Moon Elemine said at last. He let out a long breath. "It would not do to awaken you or send you to a battle you know nothing of without telling you how we came to this point." He lifted his hands and purple power swirled up to form the image of an empty galaxy. "In the beginning, Ceres was a barren and empty place. There was nothing here. Then, one day, the Light met the Dark, and shadows were formed. From those shadows came the Shadow Elemine.

"She looked upon this empty world and loved it with such force that she called up the elements that blended to become that of the power of Love. Fire for passion. Air for caresses. Sand for generosity. Water for life. Sun for pleasure. And the Moon for comfort. Life came to Ceres then and it was beautiful."

"Humans began to dream of this beautiful place," Air picked up softly. "They dreamed and dreamed and longed, and one day they came over. They spread across the land and loved it, too. Many were gifted with magic for their love." Tears shimmered across her lashes. "One day, Shadow realized that there was no one to love her. She cried out to her parents, to the Light and Dark that had made her, and they did not respond. They did not need to. When Shadow turned around, she found behind her the arms waiting to hold onto her. Light and Dark had not forsaken their child. When they had given her life, they had let their power reach into infinity to create the one who would love her. The Infinity Elemine."

"What better suits love than infinity?" the Sun Elemine asked gently. "Love lasts forever. Infinity was all of the elements in the way she was, but his power was the silver color that gray became when love turned into happy ever after. As long as he loved Shadow, she had power. As long as she needed his love, he had power. When they came together in desire," he smiled, "we six Elemine were born."

The Water Elemine took a long breath. "More than we Elemine were born, in fact. Other children were born to Shadow and Infinity. Human children who continued to have children who had children and down for centuries until their souls were so beautiful, so radiant, so light, that they grew wings."

Mai caught a breath. "That's it. That's why Lightlings eventually produced the mutation to create Darklings. The potential was always there. Angels are descended of Shadow, the place of light and dark." Her lips trembled. "And that's why we . . . why we love so much. Why we have such capacity for love. Why destiny itself blessed us." She covered Alexander's hands as his arms wrapped around her. "What happened? Why do I and Alexander stand here now? How did people forget?"

"Evil came. The wars on Earth began to leech into Ceres." Sun clenched his hands together. "War abrades against love. It brings hate. It was . . . it was too much for Shadow. Rather than risk her world, she chose to sacrifice her life to seal away the evil. She bound it to the place between Ceres and Earth to stay until she could be reborn strong enough to endure. Infinity could not live without her. I suppose you could say he entered Angelic Separation. He gave his life to follow her, knowing she would need him."

"As time passed, people forgot," the Sand Elemine said simply. "It happens after enough time. People were happy. We six were able to keep the peace. When Darklings arrived, it got people curious enough to go looking, and they found Shadow and Infinity in the history of the world. It might have remained a rumor had you not been born, Alexander." She looked at him with a smile. "That rush of Infinity power under the land could not be ignored. And then there was Maitena's birth and . . . you know the rest."

Mai drew a long breath. "The evil began to threaten to break free. It triggered Alexander to be born. The love he emitted in those years he lived before me is what drew me to rebirth. I was born on the day of an eclipse. Only another eclipse could mature me, and it could only happen when I was fair to *bursting* because of years of repressed love and desire for my mate that we could do nothing about. My maturity has infuriated the evil."

"And it now hides behind the eclipse," Moon agreed. "You are a Summoner, Maitena. You are the rarest of all angels. You alone can summon us six Elemine. We will merge with you, and Alexander will then be able to summon you—for only your guardian could—and together we can save our world."

"Back then," Alexander said quietly, "we could never have destroyed the evil if only because there was no one to summon us. Elemine cannot summon themselves. That's why I am not an Elemine anymore myself." He held Mai tighter. "What needs to be done to awaken Mai? How terrible will it be?"

"Not at all," Moon promised. "She has been moving toward this day all of her life." He held out a hand. "Come, Maitena."

She smiled up at Alexander and then walked forward to take Moon's hand. He helped her up onto the altar, and she closed her eyes as the six Elemine moved into place around her. Each began to glow softly and then brighter with their elemental color. Beams of color shot forward and struck Mai, and her eyes flew wide as power tore through her soul. The mark of Shadow suddenly appeared as a series of small tattoos all down her body, and gray streaks went through her hair from root to tip. She fell to her knees as the beams stopped, and she stared woozily at the ground. "I feel drunk."

"That should fade soon," Fire promised. "When you have recovered, find the place along the sea where the shadows lengthen into shore. It is there you can raise the lost temple of Shadow and Infinity. From within, you will be able to summon us and this can finally end. Evil has no place in our world."

Alexander stepped forward and lifted Mai into his arms. She rested her head tiredly on his shoulder, and Tynan stepped up beside them. "I can return us home," he offered. "A guardian beast is always able to teleport his or her Elemine to their home."

"Please do," Alexander told him. He rubbed his cheek over Mai's hair as he felt the magic gathering around them. He wanted this to be done as soon as possible so he could focus on a future with his angel. The past did not matter. Only their future. It was long overdue to arrive. He had waited millennia for their happy ending.

Shadow on the Sea

They returned to right outside the castle itself and within the gardens where the fountain was located. Mai felt relatively steady again, and Alexander put her on her feet. As soon as his hands lifted, she gave a yelp as Eliana came out of nowhere and tackled her flat to the ground. "Gah! Eli!"

"Mai!" Eliana hugged her cousin tight around the neck and refused to let go. "I missed you! Oh my god it was so bad here without you!"

Maduin came quickly around the corner and sighed as he saw the scene. "Figures. Welcome home, Mai." He smiled at Alexander and then frowned. "Damn. You look like shit. What happened to you two?" He broke off as he realized the cloak had fallen back and the tattoos on Mai's body were visible. "Well."

"Maitena!" Alyenna came rushing through the gardens and fell to her knees to hug her daughter just as tightly. "My baby."

The wonderfully familiar feel of her mother's arms and the sense of her power made Mai relax entirely. She closed her eyes as she rested her head on Alyenna's shoulder. "I'm perfectly fine, all things considered. There was a little trouble but Alexander saved me." She looked up at her guardian with such naked love in her eyes that even the other three angels felt humbled. "He would have died for me." She sighed. "I have to go to the sea soon to end this."

"For now," Alyenna said firmly as she tugged both of her girls to their feet, "you are going to rest. You're going to eat something tasty and have a nice hot bath. Eliana, take her inside and get her into a bathtub. The one in Alexander's suite will suffice. Maduin, get her some food."

Maduin grinned slightly. Being married to a princess and therefore effectively being a prince himself had in no way stopped his surrogate mother-in-law from ordering him around. He didn't mind. "Yes'm." He ushered the two female angels ahead of him as he headed toward the castle.

Alyenna promptly rounded on Alexander. "I want a fall wedding," she told him. "And I need at least five months to plan it. It's going to be big and beautiful because my daughter is the most beautiful creature in the world." Her tone dared anyone to argue. "That means you need to propose to her within the next few months. No later than our second spring."

He smiled. "I have only been waiting for her to reach final maturity and confirm what we knew to be true before I asked her for her hand." He went down onto one knee and bowed his head. "I will love and cherish her for all of her life."

"You already have," she whispered. "Rise, Alexander." She hugged him tightly for a moment. "You make her happy. I love you for that alone." She let him go and then sighed. "I really want a granddaughter."

"We'll work on that," he promised with a grin. "Are you looking to drive Anthony and Malthus crazy?"

She grinned and patted his cheek. "It's what we Everbird women do. We keep our men on their toes. Now go." She watched him walk away and then leaned against her mate as he came up behind her. "Why do I still feel as if something terrible may happen, Mal?" she whispered. "I just can't shake it off."

"They'll get through." He kissed her temple. "Let's go start planning a wedding. I say we make Anthony hold the reception. He's always bitching that he doesn't get to throw enough parties." It made her laugh as he had hoped, and they headed into the castle together.

While Maduin went to get food, Eliana escorted Mai down to where Alexander's suite was located. "I got to oversee moving all of your things," she noted cheerfully. "Gee, it isn't at *all* convenient that Aunt Alyenna had all along given him the three-room suite that was normally reserved for the heir and his or her mate until they were crowned."

Mai snorted softly. "I admit, as I got older, I wondered about that myself. I take it the third room is now my dressing chamber?"

"And the second room is now your shared receiving room where you can visit with people or just relax. The bedroom actually got a makeover as well. Alexander left instructions. Can I mention that I'm a tiny bit jealous you've got the most ridiculously romantic person in the world for a destined mate?"

With that said, Mai was not at all surprised to see what would be her new bedroom and discover it had been redone in dark, rich hues of gray, silver, and chocolate. The bed was the same but it had new feather covers and silk sheets.

Little sparkly things that she loved to collect were scattered in places in a way that felt lived in without feeling cluttered. The room felt both masculine and feminine and entirely *theirs*. Not his. Not hers. Theirs. She sighed gustily. "Envy me. It's absolutely deserved."

She headed into the bathing room and grimaced as Eliana helped her peel off the tunic and the ruined clothes beneath. She still had a few lingering wounds she hadn't healed and she was still filthy. She took care of the healing while her cousin ran hot water in the massive tub. It felt strange to look in the mirror and see the tattoos. They ran down both sides of her body from scalp to toe. On the left, they were dark. On the right, they were light.

"You'll be okay," Eliana said softly, bringing her gaze. "I absolutely believe it." She gently kissed Mai and then slipped from the room.

Mai scrubbed off all of the dirt in the shower and washed her hair and then gratefully got into the tub to soak away the aches. A soft, infinite power brushed over her skin, and she smiled without opening her eyes. "I'm wallowing."

"You do it quite well." Alexander leaned in the doorway and smiled. "Let me grab a shower and I'll scrub your back for you."

She peeked one eye open to watch as he

undressed and got into the shower. She sighed long and contentedly. She liked her mate naked. He was even better when he was naked and wet. When he stepped out again, she watched a few drops slide down his muscular body. She wouldn't have minded following their path with her lips. Maybe later.

The tub was more than big enough for two of them since it was more like a hot tub. He got in and then pulled her over into his arms. She tugged at his shoulders, and he obligingly turned around. Her fingers slowly traced down the scar softly. She could almost literally feel the love inside it. He truly meant it when he said he bore it proudly. She wrapped her arms around his shoulders and pressed against his back for a moment.

He turned around again and held her in return. "I'm still here," he reminded her gently. "I will love you until the end of time itself."

She kissed him fiercely for that and heat flared sharply. She pulled back with wide eyes and then gave a yelp of laughter as he pulled her onto his lap. "You can't seduce me in the tub! We'll get water everywhere."

"That's what Water magic is for, butterfly."

She sighed and conceded the point as his mouth moved slowly over her skin. "You still owe me a tumble on a rug."

They later playfully toweled each other dry, and he helped her brush out her hair. Dinner sat waiting for them in their receiving room, and she ate her entire share and even a bit of his. He didn't mind at all. When he returned from taking the tray to the hall, he found her wrapped in one of his shirts. She was perched on the window seat and watching the moon in the distance. It was the only light left for Ceres. It seemed oddly ironic when the Moon was technically the Dark element of the world. The Sun encompassed Light.

He sat across from her and studied her face. "Mai."

"Just thinking. I don't want to stay here tonight, Alex. I don't know why. Maybe I'm afraid I'll chicken out if I have to say goodbye to everyone tomorrow. Might feel too much like it really is goodbye, like we may not come home. I'm willing to give my life if it will save everyone, but I don't want to." She frowned. "Is that selfish?"

"No." He cupped her cheek gently. "You love," he said tenderly. "You can't bear hurting those you love. Your death would devastate more than just me." He got to his feet. "Let's get dressed. I want to take you somewhere. It will get us at least partway to our goal."

She blinked at him but didn't argue. She pulled on warm clothes suitable for travel and then smiled when he wrapped his cloak around her shoulders. "I'm just fine." She laughed when he picked her up to carry her. "What's with this lately?"

"Practice for when you're pregnant and I have to carry you everywhere."

"Don't you *dare*. Josh will never let me live it down."

"It'll be me or your Talia, angel. Or the rest of the guardians. In fact, I'm fairly sure anyone who thinks they can get away with it—i.e., they're bigger than you—will probably try to put you on a cushion and carry you around."

She couldn't argue with him when she knew he was right. Her only consolation would be having her mother to run interference. She rested her head on his shoulder as he carried her to the stables where he could get a horse for them. Only one, she noticed, but she didn't mind riding in front of him. There was nowhere she wanted to be more than in his arms.

They left a different direction from the kingdom and made their way across farmlands toward the open plains. Further beyond that lay the shore of the sea. It was not truly that far away. Mai had been there many times. It was one of her favorite places because of the raw nature it offered.

They dismounted on the beach, and she

walked out toward the waves until they were just teasing her feet. She pulled off her shoes and then smiled as the spray washed over her toes. She turned and smiled at Alexander as he came up beside her. "I needed this. It was always my favorite place. I guess we now know why. How many times have you brought me here so I can breathe?"

"Many," he admitted. "I have so many memories of you running down the beach toward me. You would run away first, but you could only get so far before you ran back to bring me with you."

"I've always only wanted to be with you. My favorite memories are of being here with you, and when you would tell me stories. I have copies of everything you ever wrote. My most precious treasures."

"Let's walk here, and I'll tell you another story." He brought her fingers to his lips. "You'll like this one."

"I like all of your stories." She leaned her head against his shoulder as they walked slowly along the beach. The sand was warm and so was the breeze. Cold could never touch her if he was there beside her.

"There was once," he began softly, "a wave smaller than all the others in the ocean. She could never quite seem to reach the shore. She tried and tried, but she just couldn't reach. One night as she lamented her sadness, she felt the moon shining on her. 'Come with me,' he said. 'Let me show you the way.' But the wave was scared and hid behind her bigger family members.

"The next night, she again crept out to try to find the shore. Again, she could not reach. And, again, the moon shone down and said, 'Come with me. Let me show you the way.' She looked up at him and asked 'Why?' The soft light burned more and wrapped her within its arms. 'Because I love you,' he said. She reached out, and the moon brought her to the shore where she could roll on the sands and laugh and play. With the dawn, she went home. For every night after, she would come out to play, and the moon would bring her to the shore where they could laugh and love."

She felt tears sliding down her cheeks. She didn't need to ask to see the analogy. "You're so unfair to me."

"I love you, angel." He stopped and turned her to face him. The moonlight slid over her face, and she burned with the radiant light that he could never get enough of seeing. He slowly brought her hand to his lips and then slid a bracelet over her fingers and down to her wrist. "Marry me, butterfly. Be mine for another few millennia."

She threw her arms around his neck and

went up on her toes to kiss him with all her love. "Yes yesyes!" she breathed against his lips. "Yes, always!" Her laughter rang out joyously as he swung her around in a dizzying circle. "My Alex. My hero, my guardian. *My everything!*"

He slowly lowered her to her feet and removed the cloak from around her shoulders. He threw it out across the sand and then gently carried her down to it. "You didn't even look at your engagement gift," he teased her.

She obligingly looked and her lips trembled. A small gray stone was set into the center of a silver heart strung on a chain of rainbow links. "It's beautiful."

"It's my heart," he told her, "and you're at the center of it." He kissed her again with a generosity that had her hands falling weakly to the cloak beneath them. "Your mother wants a fall wedding," he murmured.

"Fall's the best time for royal weddings."

By the time dawn came, they were sitting together along the shore watching for the eclipsed sun to rise. As it did, shadows began to crawl across the sea in a straight line toward where they sat. Mai slowly got to her feet and walked down toward the seething waters. The waves washed over her feet and then steadily calmed. It took just a moment before the ocean sat flat and motionless. When she stepped forward again, she walked across the top of the water with only tiny ripples to show where she touched. Her wings opened on a surge of power and blew her hair back and into a wild tangle.

Into the eerie silence came her power. Time froze, and the scenery changed to gray. She lifted her hands to shoulder height and then leaned back until her long hair brushed the surface of the water and her hands stretched toward the gray sky. The streaks in her hair glimmered and glowed. A soft breath was all she took before she began to sing, her voice rising and falling in an undeniable call that could never be refused.

A glow appeared not far away in the ocean as the sea began to froth. Her eyes turned gray with her power as her voice rose stronger, and feathers fell from her wings to fill the air. They swirled back toward her lover and then out across the sea, circling the sea as it began to split open violently.

Still singing, she threw her head back and poured more power into her voice. The sea surged back and forth as waves swept up around her body but never got close enough to touch. From the focal point where the storm was awakening, the sound of something immense moving was starkly audible.

The pyramid rose from the depths of the sea. It pushed itself into the air higher and higher until it stood nearly a hundred feet tall at the highest point. The length of each wall was at least the same, and the entire structure was made of the purest gray and silver seashell. The gray was iridescent in the light, rippling with light and dark in a way not dissimilar from Mai's eyes.

Seawater streamed down from the top of the temple and created large waves that rolled under Mai's feet and lifted her high in the air. A walkway rose from under the surface as well, and when it was solidly in place, the waves brought her back down until she was standing securely on the top. As her feet touched solid ground, her voice slowly faded away and time started once more.

Alexander slowly walked down toward her, and her wings briefly reached back to wrap around him in a quick hug. "I didn't know you could stop time," he murmured.

"Only briefly. Byproduct of all the elemental power. You've probably got some interesting abilities too." She walked forward down the walkway, and the doors opened at her approach. The maze within was expected and also not a concern. The route was engraved inside both of their souls.

A final room stood beyond the maze, sealed

by doors bearing the symbols of Infinity and
Shadow. They both lightly touched their symbol,
and the doors slid silently open. Torches flared
along the walls and they found themselves within
a very similar room to what had been within the
Temple of the Elemine. Seven unlit candles
circled the two altars within the center. She
moved to stand between them and then looked at
Alexander and nodded. He moved back and drew
his dagger. Infinity power lengthened it into a
sword, and he held the blade before his face for a
moment in salute.

Deliberately, tauntingly, alluringly, she began
to start and stop time over and over again. There
was no more clear way of stating her presence.
No quicker way to bring out the evil than to
abrade against it with the one thing it loathed
most: the power of love that she represented.
On. Off. On. Off. On. She played with time like
a child playing with a light switch.

A sudden horrendous scream of fury rose
on the air. Disgusting black tar began to seep
through the cracks and pores of the temple and
drip down inside. It brought with it the familiar
acrid scent of unnatural death and murder. The
scent of evil. Venomous jaws and cavernous eyes
formed within the mass as it hissed, "Shadow. I
will erase your filthy legacy once and for all."

"Yeah, cute." She lifted a brow. "Really? Am

I really supposed to be afraid of you? I'm an angel. I've been through an Unfurling, an Awakening, a Flare, and a delayed final maturity. I also went through puberty. You barely register a two on that scale."

"You think you can handle me alone?"

"Actually, I thought I'd bring some friends." Magic swelled up around her body, and she whirled to release a stream of fire at a candle. "Holy Elemine of Fire, burn away all barriers!" She swung around, and wind shot at another. "Holy Elemine of Air, blow down the enemy!" Warm soil to a third. "Holy Elemine of Sand, bury the past!" Water to the fourth. "Holy Elemine of Water, wash away the enemy!" Blazing light to a fifth. "Holy Elemine of Sun, blind all evil!" Raw darkness to the sixth. "Holy Elemine of Moon, eclipse the enemy!"

The candles lit, and the six Elemine swirled into appearance near them with a translucence to their forms to imply that they had become wholly of their power. Alexander lifted a hand and silver magic flew from his palm to the final candle. "Holy Elemine of Shadow, reset the hour and restore love!"

Mai instantly turned translucent as her fellow Elemine as her physical form was lost. The familiar mark of Shadow appeared on her forehead, and her eyes went solid gray. The other six Elemine flew forward and merged into her body, and she flew toward Alexander. Her hands briefly touched his face, though he did not feel her, and then she merged into him. He could feel her moving through his soul, and her power became his.

The mark of Infinity briefly appeared on his forehead as he gave a shout and rushed forward. The evil mass, too shocked to move, splatted against the walls with the first strike. It immediately shrieked and tried to engulf him. His skin began to glow, and the evil recoiled with a pained screech. Holy power that was both gray and silver moved over his body as he slowly lifted a hand. Mai's magic and his blended together, and power that was both Shadow and Infinity formed at his palm. When he fired it, he also fired Mai. She shot forward like a bullet and plowed into the evil mass. Its screams rose higher and higher until Alexander had to drop his sword to cover his ears.

The holy power consumed the evil and blew apart in a shockwave that seemed to rush across the entire world. The scent of evil disappeared and the air felt cleaner. The windows overhead were suddenly filled with bright sunlight as the eclipse harmlessly passed. A welcome quiet fell.

Alexander started to step toward where Mai was hovering when the other six Elemine separated from her and surrounded her. The absolute sadness on their faces made his mouth go dry, and his palms begin to sweat. "Maitena." He tried to reach for her, but his hand passed right through her arm.

She closed her eyes as Air gently hugged her. "I am sorry," Moon said softly. "We did not tell you the whole truth, Alexander. We Elemine . . . we existed only to destroy evil. There is no more need for our presence. With evil gone, all Elemine must fade. You . . . you are not an Elemine. You can't fade. But . . ."

He slowly shook his head. "No!" He tried again and again but he could not touch Mai. Tears welled and poured down her cheeks silently. "You can't take her from me!" he shouted. "How could you think I'd ever live without her?! I can't!"

She buried her face in her hands on a broken sound, and Air held her tighter. Sand and Water moved forward to hold her as well, and Moon could only say again, "I am sorry. As long as she is an Elemine, she must fade with us."

"No!" Mai burst out. She flew toward Alexander and tried to hold him though he felt nothing. "I'll come back!" she shouted. "I'll find a way to come back! Wait for me, Alex!" She reached out desperately as Water and Sun slowly pulled her away. "Alex, wait for me! Please!

Promise!"

"I'll wait forever!" he shouted. Magic swelled around him and blinded him. When he could see again, he was standing on the shore of the sea. He stared blindly at the temple as it slowly crumbled and fell into the sea. Even the shadows slowly seemed to melt away until it was as if nothing had ever been there.

Tearing, agonizing pain began to spread through his heart and soul as he felt Mai ripped out of him by the root. She was gone. Her laughter, her voice, and the joyous presence she always brought. Gone. His beautiful angel. Gone. Broken, he could only lower his head as he fell to his knees and let the tears come. He would try to wait however long he could. He had to try! They had come too far to be torn apart now.

He was still kneeling there in the sand when Eliana and Maduin found him, and neither could find anything they could say. Destiny could be a cruel mistress sometimes.

6
Shadow of my Love

Time slipped slowly past. The world had been saved, but there was no more laughter. Crystal and Chalice alike were quiet and solemn and grieving. It took months before people began to pick up their lives and finally accept that their princess was gone. The royal families themselves had to force themselves to resume their daily lives. It was hardest within Chalice for not only had they lost their beloved princess, but they also had to watch her mate slowly begin to fade away.

Alexander did not eat. He barely slept if at all. All life had left his eyes. He would spend hours upon hours in the tower where his angel had once slept. If he was not there, he was in the library, feverishly writing down the tales she had loved. He would restlessly wander the halls of the castle at night. Sami or Maduin took turns being nearby at all times in case he did anything stupid. Eliana attached herself to his side and tried to give him someone, anyone, to focus on.

He continued to exist. It could not be said he continued to live. Another month ticked by. Even Alyenna and Malthus began to have trouble believing their daughter would return. The Temple of the Elemine in the forest had disappeared, and nothing but completely crumbled ruins remained. Only Josh, Eliana, and Alexander continued to believe. Then, finally, Josh was forced to let go. Laila could only hold him as he grieved for his best friend.

On the day when even Eliana finally gave up, Alyenna looked up at the tower and saw Alexander at the window. He had lost twenty pounds. Dark circles were always under his eyes. His eyes had lost their color and you could not feel his magic. He seemed to have aged dramatically. It was like looking at her sister all over again.

Her fingers locked together as she went into the throne room. To a servant near, she said quietly, "Fetch me Maduin and Sami." She stood silently in the middle of the room and stared at the painting on the opposing wall. Her daughter's laughing smile ripped into her heart. When the door opened behind her, she said without turning, "Leave the royal guardians with me."

The room cleared except for the two guardians, and they exchanged a long look before squaring their shoulders and walking forward. "You sent for us, Majesty?" Maduin said softly. The formality was his acknowledgement that he knew whatever was discussed was of critical importance.

Alyenna slowly turned around. "I must ask you to do the hardest thing any guardian is ever asked to do." Her eyes closed. "She's gone." Her voice shook against her will. "We believed. We prayed. We hoped. We have not been answered. She is gone. I can't," her voice broke, "I can't bear any longer Alexander's suffering. He is already dying. I must ask one of you to end his Separation."

Maduin opened his mouth but Sami held up an arm in front of him. "I accept the honor of this duty," she said quietly. "Alex is my best friend. No one will end his Separation but me." She gave a deep bow and then straightened and walked out of the throne room with her back straight.

As she walked slowly through the castle toward the tower, the servants began to weep. They all knew. They knew where she was going and why. She slowly climbed the steps of the tower and silently pushed open the door at the top. Alexander had not moved from the window. She could not see or feel his magic, could barely even sense his life with her healing power.

She stepped into the tower and let the door shut. Her hand lowered and slowly drew the revolver she wore on a holster around her right leg. "Alex." She kept her voice calm. "You know I love you."

Alexander slowly looked at her and saw his friend calmly lifting the revolver. He got to his feet without a word and turned to face her. Only gratitude moved through him. He couldn't take it anymore. Mai would not come back. He would go to meet her on the other side. He closed his eyes and held out his arms. Peace. Finally. Peace.

Music began to spill in the open windows on a soft wind. Both guardians froze, and Sami slowly lowered the gun. The wind swirled slowly around Alexander. And, into the stillness, a familiar sultry voice began to sing softly.

Where have the waves gone to now?
I'm still standing on the shore I left that night
Where is the sea and sky now?
Bring them back to me and set me free

Alexander nearly knocked Sami over as he tore past his friend. He didn't even see the gunslinger following him. Hope had begun to pound inside his broken heart. The music followed him, danced in his ears. He could not deny its call. She was summoning him.

I stand here shivering with loneliness
Wrap your arms around me and warm my soul

Voices were beginning to raise in wonder and mutual hope as they heard the song. Alyenna gave a little cry as she rushed out of the throne room. "Prepare a horse!" she shouted at a servant. "*Hurry*! He must go to her!" Malthus grabbed her, and she turned into his arms on a sob. "He needs to bring her home!"

Forever my love, my heart is yours
Sweep me away from everything so cold
Forever your love, your heart is mine
This is a love that will bring back the sea

Alexander reached the stable to find a horse waiting for him. He barely spared the young stable hand a single look as he leapt into the saddle and tore out of the structure. He felt her. She was calling him. She needed him. Nothing would stop him from finding her and bringing her home!

Where does the sun lead us to now?
I can't continue walking without you there
When will the moon whisper of our love?
It will tell the tale a thousand years from now

The shadows hid my painful loneliness
Reach in and bring me back to life

He raced toward the shore of the sea in the distance. He could see a gray light beginning to swirl in the sky. When he reached the sand, he flew down from the saddle and ran desperately toward the waves. The wind continued to whip around him and tug at his hair and clothes as he stared, breath held, at the gray light forming in the sky. He could *feel* her. He could feel her beautiful shadowy power seeping into his broken soul and beginning to put him together again.

Forever my love, my heart is yours
Sweep me away from everything so cold
Forever your love, your heart is mine
This is a love that will bring back the sea

Forever my love, my heart is yours
This is our chance at eternity together
Forever your love, your heart is mine
Let our love sweep away all pain of the past

The light exploded outward and left behind a delicate figure with blue-black hair, silver eyes, and glorious gray wings. There were no Elemine marks on her body at all, but she did not glow in the light, as an angel should. He held up his arms, and she flew down into them on a broken sob that echoed the one inside his soul. Her power reached for him as desperately as his reached for her, and their souls fused together once more. Her halo blazed into appearance and reached out to consume him as well. Shadow and Infinity power met and meshed and went on forever.

"Maitena." He fell to his knees in the sand with her still clutched in his arms. The feel of her arms and wings wrapping around him was heaven. "Butterfly."

She lifted her tear-streaked face and smiled at him tremulously. "I gave it up. I sacrificed my Elemine power. Without that, I am only a Lightling with a Shadow element, just as you are a human with an Infinity element. The Elemine no longer exist. Only me. Only you. I can stay with my guardian if he wants me."

He bore her down onto the sand, and his mouth rushed over her face hungrily. Their tears stung both their skin. "Are you mad?" he demanded shakily. "I will *never* let you go again! If I ever let you out of my sight for five minutes, it will be a miracle!"

She reached for him a bit feverishly, and their mouths met and clung. Pain had rushed away in joy. Despair had turned to greedy desire. Too long. She had been too long without him by her side. She crawled into his soul, and his power swept over her wonderfully. She would never, ever tell him the nightmare she had crawled through to strip herself of Elemine power. Only the other six Elemine had allowed her to survive. Every agonizing moment had been worth it to be there in her mate's arms once again. "Alex." She kissed him as deeply as she could until she knew he could taste her soul. She could certainly taste his.

Much further up the shore, Eliana watched the lovers embracing and calmly used her Sun magic to raise up walls of sand around them for some privacy. She dusted off her hands and then turned to smile at Maduin and Alyenna. "Fall wedding? I think we can just make it if we plan fast."

They made it. The leaves were just starting to change to beautiful golds and reds as Mai and Alexander were wed under the arbor in the garden. They should have walked alone together down the aisle, but Mai had made one small request: that the train of her gown be carried by the large gray wolf who had been by her side since childhood and would stay with her through eternity. She was not an Elemine anymore, but he did not care. She was his mistress. He would have no other.

Josh and Eliana stood by Mai's side as her attendants, and Sami and Maduin stood with Alexander as his. Josh caught Laila's eye in the audience and winked at her. They had postponed their own wedding only because Josh had wanted

Mai at his side, but Laila had opted to push it just a bit further out to make room for one *far* more overdue.

There was nothing that could have made the day more perfect, except for one tiny, little, announcement the royal judge got to make at the very end. As Mai and Alexander turned to face the crowd, he said clearly, "Chalice Kingdom, before you are your future queen and king. They will lead us into a future full of joy and hope." A smile entered his voice. "And it is with much pleasure that I now announce the coming birth of the next heir to the throne. In eight months, we will celebrate the royal birth of the next crown princess."

Cheers ripped through the air until the entire world seemed to be vibrating within them. The judge looked at Mai and said, "Your Highness, you may claim your mate."

"I think she already did," Josh noted dryly, and set off riots of laughter.

Mai turned, shoved her bouquet into his arms, and then whirled and leapt into Alexander's arms to kiss him with all the love and desire inside her angelic soul. When his arms closed around her, she knew her entire world was right there.

They did indeed hold the reception at the Crystal Kingdom. Anthony and Gillian were more than glad to throw open the doors and help celebrate. But the king did tell his best friend dryly, "*You* get to host Josh and Laila!"

Mai danced until her feet were aching, and after every dance, she always rushed right back to her husband's side. There was nowhere else she wanted to be. As he watched her dancing circles around a laughing Robert, Alexander felt Sami come up beside him. He turned and looked at his friend and then smiled. "Sami . . . thank you. For loving me enough to almost do what you were willing to."

She clapped him on the shoulder. "I'll call us even if I don't have to deal with your daughter's Unfurling." She smiled when Mai joined them and eyed her suspiciously. "Yes?"

"Just what were you willing to do?" she demanded.

"That's a secret." Sami tapped her nose and then walked away with a light whistle.

Mai scowled at Alexander. "Don't think I don't already know even though you won't tell me. Eliana has a big mouth."

"Indeed." He trailed a finger over her cheek. Impending motherhood suited her. Her halo had grown brighter, and she always seemed glow from the inside out rather than just on the outside. "I think it's time I went ahead and did something I keep promising to do."

"Oh?"

"It has to do with a rug." He scooped her up and tossed her over his shoulder as he strode for the exit. "Excuse us. My wife and I are starting our honeymoon early."

"Don't you dare!" she yelped. She kicked her feet and tried to not start laughing. "Damn it, Alexander! I'll never live this down! Oooh, you're so going to get it for this!"

Amid the laughter as the couple left, Malthus grinned at Anthony and asked, "Am I the only one hoping that their daughter is *exactly* like Mai?"

"Cheers!" the entire reception chorused as they raised their glasses in the air. Nothing would have made anyone happier than to have another little angel just like her sassy, sultry, loving, and amazing mother.

She was, quite truly, the love that held the world together. The very reason why Ceres was heaven, and why angels called it home.

The happy ending had finally arrived.

Author's Notes

I hope you enjoyed SHADOW ON THE SEA and visiting my magical world of angels in this first tale of my Descendants series. There's more to come as Maitena and Alexander's daughter will have quite a future of her own, and more than Ceres might be at stake this time . . .

Did you enjoy this story? Please leave me a review on Amazon.com. I would love to hear about your experience in Ceres!

If you'd like to keep up with me online, you can follow me on Facebook (www.facebook.com/stacyjgarrett/) or on my website (www.stacyjgarrett.com). You can sign up for my mailing list from either location to get the first news on new books, behind-the-scenes info, and even exclusive artworks.

On the next page is a sneak peek into THE CARMICHAEL FILE, the next book in the 3rd District story, coming 2016 from PDMI Publishing. The first book, THE SHAUGHNESSY FILE, is currently available on Amazon.com (under my pen name Etta Jean).

Keep falling in love, readers. It's the strongest magic alive.

Stacy J Garrett

IS SHE THE FAIREST ONE OF ALL?

He tuned everything out around him, only vaguely listening to the doors opening and closing. He had been trying for a week to design a faerie princess for the next game he was working on. He just couldn't picture her in his mind. Kind and beautiful but spirited. Waving a wand, he thought with humor, but not to cast magic. She was horrible at magic. A fireball might turn into an inferno or never even light a candle.

A feminine giggle cut across his thoughts and instantly stole his attention. His heart gave a wild clench in his chest and then kicked into overdrive. He looked up in shock to see the security guard offering his arm to a young woman trying to put her shoe back on. The guard was smiling widely and said something that had the young woman giggling again. The sound seemed to dance teasingly through Taylor's heart and soul.

As if sensing his gaze, she looked right at him and gave him an impish smile. The entire world went away from around him in a wash of color. There she was. His faerie princess, smiling at him in a rain-splashed suit the color of fresh snow.

Her hair was the same, a wild tumble of white curls that framed a face too beautiful to be real. Her eyes were an unusual shade of purple-gray, like the storm clouds that brought thunder and lightning. She was tiny, only barely over five feet in height, and had a slender frame and gently curved figure. She was stunning. Breathtaking. If she had sprouted faerie wings, he wouldn't have batted a lash.

About the Author

Stacy J. Garrett was made in England but born in Sacramento, California, and like the redwoods of the state, her roots have dug deep. Her destiny as a bard was somewhat inevitable. Little else can explain how she constantly told her mother tall tales so outlandish that she couldn't even get grounded for them. Her mother and grandmother had her reading by age three, and that love of a good story propelled her through so many books that Scholastic Books gave her a medal. A love of worlds created by others eventually brought out the desire to create her own, and she has never looked back.

Stacy has seen both good and evil in her life, and her stories, like life, have no half measures. Even in a fantasy world of dragons and faeries, even in a modern city where magic abounds, she knows that the constants of real emotion never change. Dreams come true, love can be found at first sight, princesses can rescue their princes, and maybe there really can be happily ever after. Her happy endings never come without cost, though, for she truly believes we can't appreciate the good and the joy without the bad and the pain along the way.

Her current haunt is a comfy house in her beloved Sacramento where she wrangles four feline fur-kids and consumes peppermints like mana in order to balance a calendar filled with more creative venues than a sane person should realistically undertake. If she's not chained to her desk, she's stomping through the scenery in search of equally fantastical photographs.